"We're going to have a baby, Mrs. Summers."

Carrie grinned at her husband until the reality hit her. "We have to get ready!" The mother's due date is in three weeks. "There's so much to do—a nursery, a layette…"

"We'll get it all done," Brian said soothingly. "In fact, we can probably get lots of things done in one night. Why don't you start looking into baby furniture, pick out what you want, and we'll go look at it all together."

Carrie couldn't believe Brian was going to be home early enough to spend time with her, shopping, discussing their baby's birth. This child was going to change their lives…for the better.

When Brian bent his head to kiss her, Carrie felt tears coming to her eyes. His lips were gentle on hers at first, then he deepened the kiss. She felt his intensity and hunger and need.

As he broke away, she felt shaken. "I'm looking forward to tonight."

"So am I," Carrie said in response. She could only hope that everything would be okay now, and the problems they'd had in the past would disappear once they held their son.

KAREN ROSE SMITH

The award-winning author of forty-five published novels, Karen Rose Smith loves to write. She began putting pen to paper in high school when she discovered poetry as a creative outlet. Also writing for her high school newspaper, intending to teach someday, she never suspected crafting emotional and romantic stories would become her life's work!

Married for thirty-three years, Karen Rose was excited to be asked to participate in the LOGAN'S LEGACY continuity series and pen a story line about a married couple. Believing in commitment and the power of vows, she drew on her own experiences to develop Brian and Carrie Summers. As she wove in the suspense continuity threads, the project became even more intriguing.

Karen Rose and her husband reside in Pennsylvania with their two cats, Ebbie and London. Readers can e-mail Karen Rose through her Web site at www.karenrosesmith.com or write to her at P.O. Box 1545, Hanover, PA 17331.

LOGAN'S LEGACY

A PRECIOUS GIFT
KAREN ROSE SMITH

Silhouette Books

Published by Silhouette Books
America's Publisher of Contemporary Romance

Special thanks and acknowledgment are given
to Karen Rose Smith for her contribution
to the LOGAN'S LEGACY series.

 SILHOUETTE BOOKS

ISBN 0-373-61389-X

A PRECIOUS GIFT

Visit Silhouette Books at www.eHarlequin.com

Printed in U.S.A.

Be a part of

ℒogan's ℒegacy

*Because birthright has its privileges
and family ties run deep.*

One woman lived with a secret that threatened
her marriage. Would she find the courage to
face the man she loved?

Carrie Summers: She had a past she couldn't
share with Brian. With the mounting tension over her
inability to conceive, Carrie didn't know how much
more their marriage could take. She just hoped that
her precious husband would love her no matter what.

Brian Summers: He loved Carrie so much, and they
wanted to have a child together. But infertility issues
were taking a heavy toll on their relationship. Could
he convince her to trust him—that nothing could
change his feelings for her?

A teenager in trouble, **Lisa Sanders** wanted to
help the Summers family. But should she be able
to help herself?

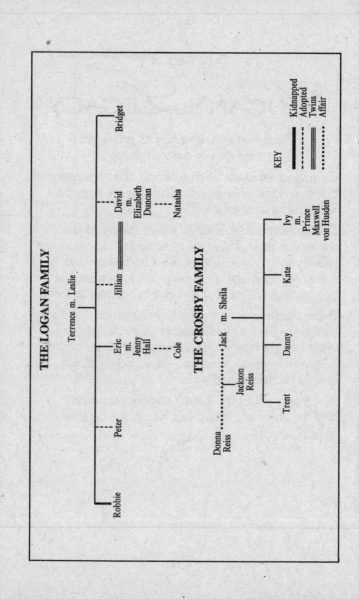

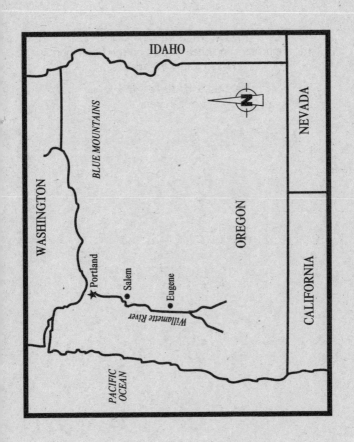

To Carolyn, Susan and Edie—
my supporters and cheerleaders on this book journey.
I'm so glad we're friends.

To my husband, Steve—thank you.
Love, Karen.

One

Carrie Summers paced the blue-and-white tiled general reception area in Children's Connection. Her husband was fifteen minutes late for their appointment at the agency, and she was afraid that meant Brian had changed his mind about adopting. They'd answered question after question and submitted to a home study that was now finished. This was their last meeting with the caseworker before they were put into the system.

Brian was never late.

He was a man of his word—a man she'd always been able to depend upon. But for the past three years of their five-year marriage, tension had built between them. When they'd married, Carrie had been so in love, so absolutely sure their wedding vows would be everlasting. However, she had a secret, and the repercussions of that secret were pushing them apart.

If only Brian could embrace the idea of an adoption wholeheartedly. If only Brian could accept an adopted child as his own.

"Are you ready?" a deep male voice asked.

She'd been watching the double glass doors leading outside to the unusually sunny January day. Rain always fell on Portland, Oregon, this time of year. Now she swung around and faced the man whose voice always vibrated through her like a heartfelt song.

"Where did you come from?" she asked with a smile, trying to hide her anxiety over his lateness.

"There was something I had to do before this meeting."

Brian Summers was six foot two, muscular, incredibly fit and more handsome than any man Carrie had ever seen. His thick tawny hair waved over his brow, and he kept it in a clipped style to suit his image—that of a real-estate developer on the go, a millionaire who cared less about his appearance than the powerhouse deals he brokered. When they'd first met, she'd known he'd spoken to her at that cocktail party because she'd looked like the model she'd been. Although her black dress had been demure and classic, his eyes had lingered often on her dark-red hair and the angles of her face, as well as her figure. Their attraction had been mutual, and that night she'd hoped Brian could see beyond her outward appearance. He'd seemed to, and that was why she'd fallen in love with him.

"You've had a meeting in the hospital?" Land development deals didn't usually begin at Portland General.

"No, nothing like that."

Just then, the door to the inner offices opened and a middle-aged brunette smiled at them. "Are you Carrie and Brian Summers?"

They answered in unison. "Yes."

"You'll be meeting with me today." She extended her hand first to Brian and then to Carrie. "I'm Trina Bentley."

"We've gone through this whole process with Stacy Williams," Brian said with a frown.

"Yes, I know you have. Stacy's out with the flu. Since this last meeting is simply a formality, I told her I'd take it for her so we can give you the official okay and find you a baby. Come on back to my office."

In their first years together, Brian had always been solicitous of Carrie, often showing affection by a touch of his hand on her shoulder, his arm around her waist. They hadn't touched as much recently, not since the in vitro attempts had failed. Now as they walked side by side, the sleeve of Brian's suit jacket brushed her arm. She felt the jolt of his close proximity through the sleeve of her cream wool dress.

Everything about Children's Connection was bright and welcoming, including Trina's office. It was pale yellow with a bulletin board on one wall covered with pictures of children from infants to teenagers.

The caseworker motioned to the two upholstered chairs in front of her desk. "Have a seat. I promise I'll make this as painless as possible."

Carrie stole a glance at Brian. He hadn't liked discussing the details of his life with a stranger. He was a private man, and he hadn't appreciated answering questions about his work habits, family history and finances. The poking and prodding into his personal and business life had rankled. Yet today he seemed calmer, more accepting about the whole thing, and Carrie wondered why.

Opening the folder on her desk, Trina glanced over

the pages as if she were familiar with them. "I've read through everything including the home-study report." Leaning back in her chair, she focused her hazel eyes on Carrie. "You've been through a lot."

Panicking, Carrie felt her mouth go dry. Could this woman somehow know...?

Trina went on, "You had the procedure to try to unblock your tubes, two in vitro attempts, and I suspect the usual temperature taking and ovulation charts before all this began."

Carrie nodded.

"You must want a child very much."

"I—we do."

Although Trina's gaze was kindly, she obviously had a mission today as she continued. "As the oldest of four sisters, you did quite a bit of mothering. Some women who have that responsibility thrust on them seem to run in the other direction. But the psychologist's evaluation suggests that although you haven't had much practice since then, you're a nurturing woman who can't wait to take care of someone again."

"That's true," Carrie agreed honestly.

"She also noted that you haven't modeled in three years. It seems you've filled your time with working for charities, volunteering at the hospital in the children's ward and being available whenever your husband needs you."

Now Brian shot Carrie a curious look. They'd interviewed with the psychologist separately as well as together. This had come up during her one-on-one interview.

"Why do you need to be available for your husband?" Trina asked.

Feeling Brian shift in his seat, Carrie knew his gaze was on her. She looked directly at Trina. "Brian has a lot of social contact with clients. We often give cocktail parties and dinners, and sometimes I go out of town with him."

"Carrie has always been an asset," Brian interjected. "She's good at public relations and is easy to talk to." His tone was even, but there was an edge to it, and Carrie knew he wondered where this was going.

"I see," Trina mused. "I guess I'm concerned how you'll feel about that when a child is demanding her attention and she can't fly out of town, or maybe even hostess a dinner."

The statement was akin to a grumble of thunder when the sky was still fair.

Finally Brian replied, "Dinners and parties are often held when a child would be asleep."

"But children don't always stay asleep, and they can be as unpredictable as the weather. I suppose I'm just wondering how you'll cope with that."

Carrie could practically see Brian's shoulders tense as he replied, "Miss Bentley, I don't know exactly how we'll deal with that, but we *will* deal with it. I want a child as much as Carrie does. No couple knows for certain how their lives will be impacted by a baby. I can assure you a child of ours will always have the attention and care it needs."

"When we began evaluating you as future parents, I think you had some doubts about adopting, didn't you, Mr. Summers?"

This woman was obviously leaving no stone unturned. Carrie's heart sped up.

"Yes, I did," Brian answered honestly. "Family has

always been important to me, and I always imagined I'd have three or four kids."

"You grew up with your father."

Carrie held her breath, waiting for Brian's reaction. His childhood with Dutch Summers had been a difficult one. Dutch hadn't held one job any length of time or brought home a paycheck often. Usually he gambled it away.

"Yes." Brian's quick answer said he didn't want to go into all of this again.

But Trina didn't take the hint. "Your mother abandoned you and your father when you were seven. Miss Williams's report states your mother contacted you shortly after you were married but you have no contact with her now."

"That's right."

"There are notes here that the noncontact is your choice. Can you tell me why?"

"I told Stacy why," he responded gruffly.

"I know these questions seem prying, Mr. Summers, but extended family is important to children, too— grandmothers, grandfathers, cousins, uncles, aunts. Your wife's family is still very much connected, but your father has passed on and your mother's not in your life. Do you see that changing?"

"I don't see it changing, at least not right now. My mother left and didn't call or write for twenty-two years. If we make contact and try to start over, she could drop out of my life and a child's again. As you said, my wife is still close to her family. We *would* have an extended family."

Addressing Carrie, the caseworker asked, "How do you feel about your husband's lack of a relationship with his mother?"

Carrie *was* still close to her family, but her own relationship with her mom and dad was complicated, more so than even Brian realized. "I trust Brian's judgment," she said simply.

When Brian leaned forward, Carrie could feel the intensity in him. "I was almost late to this meeting because I made a stop at the hospital nursery to have a look at the babies. I've always dreamed of having a family *because* mine wasn't ideal. I never expected that would mean adopting a child. But as I stood there looking at the infants and their little hands, their big eyes, some of them crying, I knew I wanted a child with Carrie. If that means adoption, that's what we'll do."

Turning to his wife, he took her hand in his. "We'll have the family we've always wanted."

The tenderness in Brian's voice gave Carrie more hope than she'd had in months. For so long, she'd felt she was losing him. She couldn't tell Brian what had caused her infertility problems. If she did, he'd walk away…as Foster had. However, if they adopted, her secret would be safe and their marriage could become strong again.

Tears pricked in her eyes and Brian saw them. He squeezed her hand.

Their interview went smoothly after that. After they signed more papers, Trina assured them they'd be in the system by noon. If a birth mother chose them, she'd notify them immediately.

When Carrie emerged into the lobby again with Brian, her heart felt lighter than it had in years. She knew babies didn't "fix" marriages, yet their only problem had been her inability to bear children. This morning she'd almost felt close to her husband again, and that

was what a baby was going to do for them—bring them
even closer.

They stopped by the coatrack in the reception area
and Carrie took her off-white winter coat from the
wooden hanger. By her side, Brian lifted it from her
hands and held it. When their gazes collided, she ac-
knowledged again the one element that had drawn them
together since the night they'd met—their attraction to
each other. As she slipped one arm into the sleeve, Brian
dipped his head and his lips were very close to her temple. His aftershave smelled of pine and woods, and a
small tremble shimmered through her. She thought
about tonight, holding each other, giving in to passion
that never diminished between them no matter what
else was happening.

As he helped her with her other sleeve, she asked
hopefully, "Will you be home for dinner?"

Before Brian could answer, a lean man approached
them. Everett Baker was an accountant for Children's
Connection. Carrie had seen him now and then in the
halls of the adoption agency, which was an annex to
Portland General. A nurse who worked in the emergency room, Nancy Allen, often visited the children in
pediatrics when Carrie volunteered there, and they'd
become friends. Nancy and Everett seemed to have a
friendship, if not more than that. She'd introduced Everett to Carrie soon after he'd taken a job at Children's
Connection. While Nancy was warm, outgoing and definitely an extrovert, Everett was the opposite—reserved,
almost shy. But he was good-looking with a square jaw,
dark-brown hair and eyes. He'd never approached Carrie on his own before, though. He'd always hung back
and let Nancy do the talking.

Now he looked purposeful as he came up to them. "Mrs. Summers," he said with a half smile.

"It's Carrie, Everett. I don't think you've met my husband, Brian."

The two men shook hands. Afterward Everett shifted on his feet as if he were uncomfortable, but then he began, "I don't want to hold you up. But Nancy told me you and your husband were thinking about adopting a child."

Their intentions to adopt weren't a secret, and Carrie had told Nancy about them a few weeks ago.

"We just finished with the final interview," Brian said. In his voice, Carrie could tell there was curiosity as to why Everett Baker was interested in what they were doing.

With a quick look over his shoulder to the adoption agency offices where no one was visible, Everett continued. "I know how long the adoption process can take. When Nancy told me you were seriously interested, I thought I might help out. I have a friend who knows a lawyer and he can make private adoptions happen faster. If you're interested in adopting out of the system, it would be something to think about."

One look at Brian's face and Carrie knew what he was thinking. Her husband was a by-the-book kind of guy and would have made a great police officer as he seemed to separate black from white easily, much more easily than she could.

Speaking for both of them, Brian handled the offer casually. "Carrie and I will think about it. This is an important step in our lives. Thank you for trying to help us."

Although this discussion was serious, Carrie almost smiled. Brian was so good at handling delicate situations. He'd managed to give Everett Baker a don't-call-us, we'll-call-you message without being rude.

"I know adoption is serious," Everett agreed. "Babies are serious." He looked troubled, and then the shadows passed from his eyes as he handed Carrie a business card. "You can reach me any time at that number."

"Thank you." Carrie tucked his card into her purse.

As soon as Everett walked away, Brian shook his head. "I don't like the idea of going outside of a reputable adoption center."

"I agree…for now. Let's just see what happens in the next few months. If it goes a really long time and we haven't heard anything or been chosen by a birth mother, maybe we'll want to call Everett then."

When Brian turned to face her, Carrie could see he'd already dismissed the encounter with Everett as well as the idea of a private adoption. "You asked me if I'll be home for dinner. I won't be. I have a meeting at the Hilton." Apparently she couldn't hide her disappointment because he went on, "I'll try to be home before midnight."

Carrie knew if Brian said he'd be home before midnight, he would be.

Her husband looked as if he wanted to say more, maybe do more. Public displays of affection had gone the way of holding hands and kissing in the car at stoplights. But as if he needed some type of contact between them as much as she did, he slid his forefinger along a wave of her auburn hair that had gotten caught under her coat. Gently he pulled it free and then stepped away.

"I'll see you tonight." His voice was low and husky, making her wonder if the pictures running through her head were running through his.

"Tonight," she murmured.

A few moments later, Brian strode toward the parking garage, and she headed for the hospital. She loved reading stories to the children in pediatrics and today was her day to volunteer there. The time would pass quickly, and maybe at the end of the day she'd look at baby furniture before returning home to her big, beautiful empty house. Soon it wouldn't be empty.

Soon, she and Brian would have the family they'd always wanted.

At eleven forty-five, Brian entered his kitchen after resetting the security system. Carrie was obsessive about it. If he slid into bed without waking her, he often heard her in the middle of the night going downstairs to check it. The few times he'd questioned her about it, she'd simply said she felt safer when she was sure it was on.

Striding down a hall, Brian bypassed the first floor spare bedroom and stopped in his den. After he set his briefcase on his desk, he hit a button on the computer, saw that he had no pressing e-mails, and headed for the second floor.

The house he'd bought after he and Carrie had married projected traditional charm. When he'd shown it to Carrie for the first time, she'd just kept saying, "It's so big!"

It wasn't *that* big. The two-story foyer opened into a dining room on the right and a living room on the left. A corridor to the left of the stairs led to his den and a guest bedroom. Pocket doors separated the living room from a great room, and beyond the great room's French doors, outdoor floodlights beamed along a path leading to a gazebo-enclosed hot tub. He'd always envisioned three or four kids playing in the family room and in the yard. His gut still twisted when he thought about not being able to have kids of their own. Yet watching those babies in the nursery today…

He mounted the stairs, remembering the two-bedroom box house he'd grown up in. His father had lived there until he'd died two years ago, refusing to let Brian move him anywhere bigger. Carrie's background had been even poorer than his own because her father had been disabled from a logging accident and her mother was unskilled. They'd been on and off welfare until Carrie had begun modeling. After Carrie's mom had sent her daughter's picture to a contest in a magazine, their lives had changed drastically.

The first night he'd met Carrie, he'd been bowled over by her—her beautiful long, wavy auburn hair and porcelain skin, her big brown eyes that seemed to see into his soul. She'd looked so sophisticated and been so poised and well-spoken that he'd never suspected her background had been similar to his.

Moonlight flowed through a skylight in the hall as Brian reached the top of the stairs. Their bedroom door was invitingly ajar and a dim light glowed within. When he stepped inside the master suite, his gaze didn't sway toward the graceful columns that separated the sleeping area from a sitting room with its own fireplace. Rather it swerved unerringly toward the huge, king-sized bed. Although Carrie was five foot eight, with long graceful legs, she still seemed small and fragile in that bed.

Their triple dresser and the almost ceiling-high armoire were simply blurs as Brian quickly undressed and hung his suit in the closet. His wife was sound asleep. He could tell. When she curled on her side like that and tucked her hands under her cheek, she usually didn't stir. Why should she? It was midnight.

He'd already been at the top of his game when he'd met her and had invested and saved more money than he could ever spend. His first successful land development deal had been followed by another and then another. He'd worked hard, used his intuition as well as his wit. He'd found, bought and sold land from Hawaii to Alaska to the coast of Maine. Although he'd always worked long hours, Carrie had understood the business he was in, knowing his pager could go off at any time or he could be bothered by an international conference call in the middle of the night. Still, during their courtship and the first year of their marriage, they'd had more time for each other. He'd taken her to Aruba and the Caymans. He'd introduced her to Tuscany vineyards and the moors of Cornwall. Sometimes trips were work-related, others they'd stayed in bed as much as they'd seen the sights. But then something had happened.

They couldn't get pregnant.

Finally they'd both been tested and found Carrie's tubes were blocked. Knowing how much he'd always wanted a real family, she'd been heartsick. The doctors had offered hope that had withered rather than materialized when the procedure to correct the problem wasn't successful. Then the in vitro failed, too.

In the past few years, work had taken over more of Brian's life, and Carrie just seemed to be on the fringes of it. Although the chemistry between them had tumbled them both into a whirlwind courtship and marriage, Brian had always sensed Carrie held part of herself away from him. Much more experienced than she was, at first he'd thought it was an innocent shyness, then a natural reserve that came from her upbringing. But as having a family eluded them month after month, she'd seemed to withdraw more, and he had to admit he'd been in turmoil about all of it, too. When she'd suggested adoption, he hadn't wanted to consider it. But the tension had grown more palpable between them, and he'd finally agreed to begin the interview process.

Now...

Now as he approached the bed and looked at his wife's body under the sheet, he realized Carrie wasn't wearing a nightgown. Usually she did. Usually he enjoyed ridding her of it. The sight of her in the moonlit shadows, the idea of his skin touching hers, aroused him fully.

When she felt his weight on the bed, she came awake as if even in her dreams she'd been waiting for him. Her eyes opened and her hand fluttered out to touch him. It landed lightly on his chest. "I tried to stay awake. What time is it?"

"Midnight."

"Long day," she murmured sleepily but then came more awake and smiled at him.

The light, whispery scent of a flowery shampoo seemed to pull him closer to her. Switching off the lamp and angling on his side, he was suddenly overwhelmed by a caveman desire to make her his without gentle kisses and touches, without foreplay, with nothing but mindless need. Yet something had always kept him from doing that. Carrie's entry into his life had made him notice starlight and sunsets and orchids growing on undeveloped land. She'd awakened a protective instinct in him as well as a primitive one.

When he slid his hand into her hair, she raised her face to his.

"Are you as excited as I am about adopting this baby?" she asked softly.

"I will be. It's not real yet."

"It could happen quickly."

"Or an unwed mother could choose us early in her pregnancy, and we'd go through the whole process with her. It would take months."

"That might be even more wonderful."

His wife's voice was happy with the idea, but Brian knew that *that* scenario carried its share of hazards. What if the mother changed her mind? What if she gave birth and kept the baby? As far as he was concerned, adoption was filled with land mines. But it was their only option now except for a surrogate, and he believed that would be even more complicated.

"You're still not sold on adoption, are you?" Carrie's voice caught with worry.

"I want a family, and I want it with you." As far as he was concerned, that said it all.

Her eyes became luminous then, and he couldn't restrain the desire to kiss her. It was hot and deep and wet, and Carrie responded to it by meeting his tongue with hers, wrapping her arms around his neck, moving her body close to his. They usually took it slower but there seemed to be a desperation in both of them tonight. Their touches, kisses and caresses were filled with a yearning he couldn't define. When he entered her, she clung to him. Their bodies glistened as they climaxed.

When the ripples of pleasure from their lovemaking ended, Brian rolled away from Carrie, physically spent. More than physically spent. Something about their union tonight had shaken him. It was as if they'd been skating on a frozen lake, had felt the ice cracking beneath them, and had held on to each other just the same, denying what was happening.

Carrie slipped her hand into his and they lay there a long time. "Are you awake?" she asked in a whisper.

"Yes."

"The caterer called today while I was at the hospital to go over the menu for Saturday night. I'll finalize everything with him tomorrow. We're still having six guests?"

The dinner they were giving on Saturday would bring together his closest associates and their wives. "Yes, plus the two of us. Do you still want to fly to San Francisco with me on Wednesday to see your sister?"

"If that's all right with you."

"I'd like you to have dinner with my client and his wife."

"That's fine. Brenda has to go to work at five anyway. I'm hoping if we have a few hours alone, I can convince her to give college another try."

Carrie's younger sister Brenda was twenty now. She'd dropped out of Berkeley and an education Carrie had been funding because she'd fallen in love with an L.A. musician. It hadn't worked out and she was back in San Francisco now working behind the cosmetics counter in a department store. Brian stayed clear of giving advice to Carrie where her family was concerned. He knew nothing about sibling dynamics and when it came to parents… Carrie was polite to hers, the perfect daughter as far as he could see. There seemed to be an invisible wall between Carrie and her mother, though. Maybe he recognized it because he sometimes felt that same wall between Carrie and him.

Suddenly Brian felt restless, much too wired to go to sleep. Sliding his hand from Carrie's, he moved to the edge of the bed.

"Where are you going?"

"I have work to take care of before we go to San Francisco—a spreadsheet on property assessments."

His wife was silent and he knew why. Nothing she could say would dissuade him from going to his office downstairs.

"I'll see you in the morning," she said softly.

Standing by the side of the bed, he was so tempted to touch her again.

But then she pulled the sheet up to her shoulders and turned over.

Brian snatched up his sweatpants from the bedside chair and left the bedroom, closing the door behind him.

Two

"Are you almost ready?" Brian called up the stairs on Wednesday morning.

Lifting her cosmetics case from the dresser, Carrie took a last look in the mirror at her sea-green pantsuit and went into the hall. "I'm ready. Are you in a hurry to get to the airport?"

"I'm initiating a conference call after we get through security. I don't want to have to rush it."

Ever since Monday night when Brian had made love to her so passionately, he'd seemed to withdraw. Sometimes she didn't understand him, and she knew he didn't always understand her. She marveled how when they'd first met, they'd seemed to be able to read each other's minds. Where had that ability gone?

"I guess I'd better take along something to read if you're going to be tied up." She'd hoped they'd discuss their plans for the baby. She'd hoped—

As she descended the steps, the phone rang. Since Brian was already in the kitchen on his way to the garage with their luggage, she went to the living room and picked up the cordless phone. "Summers residence," she answered automatically.

"Mrs. Summers, it's Trina Bentley from Children's Connection."

"Hi, Trina. What can I do for you?" The caseworker probably needed yet another signature on something.

"I think I might be able to do something for *you*."

Carrie's heart began to pound. "Do you have a baby?"

Brian had returned from the garage and caught her question to the caseworker. Standing in the doorway, his gaze met hers.

"Not exactly, but a baby could be the end result."

"I don't understand."

Obviously eager to explain, Trina went on, "What we have is an unwed mother who is homeless. Her name is Lisa Sanders. She's been residing in a shelter for the past month. Yesterday she passed out, and one of her friends called the paramedics. In the emergency room, one of the nurses referred her to a social worker. When Lisa said she wanted to put her baby up for adoption, I was assigned to talk to her."

"How old is she?" Carrie asked, thinking about how scared the young woman must be without a secure roof over her head.

"Lisa is eighteen and eight months pregnant. She's been waitressing, but her blood pressure's elevated. She has to slow down for her health as well as the baby's. I gave her several portfolios to examine. She chose yours and that's why I'm calling. As you know, the adopting couple often pays for the medical expenses for the mother of the child they're going to adopt, and it would be true in Lisa's case. We also need a couple who is willing to take her in until the baby's born. Would you consider doing that?"

"I don't know." Carrie cast a worried glance at Brian. "We'd definitely be able to adopt?"

There was a short pause. "While Lisa is living with you, she could determine whether you and your husband are her choice to adopt her baby."

"I see."

"This isn't as irregular as it seems, Mrs. Summers. All types of arrangements can be negotiated between mothers giving up their children and the adoptive parents. Do you think you'd be interested?"

Carrie was more than interested. For years she'd acted as a second mother to her three sisters, and she missed taking care of someone. Since she'd stopped modeling, she'd become more involved in volunteer work but there was still a hole in her life that needed to be filled. That hole had grown bigger since Brian's success took him away from home more and more. Taking care of this teenager could fill some of the emptiness. It could also lead to the end result of becoming a mother.

"I have to talk to my husband about this. We're on our way to the airport. How soon must I give you a decision?"

"As soon as possible. Lisa's gone back to the shelter, but we'd like to get her out of there."

"I'll talk to Brian now and get back to you."

"That was Children's Connection?" he asked, sounding wary as Carrie replaced the cordless phone on its stand.

"Yes, it was Trina. We could have a baby in less than a month!" She couldn't keep the excitement from her voice. "An eighteen-year-old unwed mother, Lisa Sanders, is living in a shelter and needs a place to stay until she has her baby. She's chosen us as a possible couple. Isn't that wonderful?"

His expression and demeanor said that wasn't his assessment of the situation. "Let me get this straight. A teenager who's homeless wants to give up her baby. What do you know about her?"

"Not much...yet. But she doesn't have anywhere to go, Brian."

"We don't know where she came from or what she's been doing. We can't just bring a stranger into the house."

"Why not?"

Now he looked at her as if she'd totally lost her mind. "Because she might not be honest, she might do drugs, she might steal. Why is she on the streets? Why is she homeless? You can't make a decision like this without having the right information." He checked his watch. "And I don't have time to get it now. We have a flight to catch."

Ever since they were married, Carrie had supported Brian's career. She loved him. If it was in her power, she'd do anything to make him happy. That had included giving up modeling and being available when he needed her. Since she'd learned she couldn't have children, and since she hadn't told Brian the real reason, guilt had kept her quiet about his long hours and his reticence to adopt a child as well as about how lonely she was. Now, however, she could envision laughter filling this big house. They had so much...and she'd love to help a young girl in need, not just with a roof over her head, but with emotional support. Carrie remembered how desperately she'd needed that after the rape, after her abortion, after her world had fallen to pieces all around her.

"I want to meet her, Brian."

"I guess that will have to wait until we get back from San Francisco. Maybe you can make an appointment for Friday."

"She's homeless *now*. She needs a place to stay *now*."

His brows drew together at her unexpectedly adamant tone. "I can't cancel this trip."

"I'm not asking you to cancel it, but I don't have to go with you. If I call Brenda and explain, I know she'll understand. I can see her another time. I can go meet Lisa today."

"I was counting on you to be at dinner tonight."

"Is that really necessary? Isn't adopting a baby more important than showing me off to one of your clients?" As soon as the words were out, she couldn't believe she'd said them.

"That's the way you feel about coming to dinner with me?"

Except for keeping her secret, she'd always been honest with Brian and she knew she had to be now. "Sometimes that's the way I feel. Don't you see, Brian, that I need to be more than a wife who was once a model, more than a wife who can facilitate conversation and give great parties?"

Her attitude seemed to baffle him. "You picked a great time to bring this up."

"I'm sorry. I know you have to leave."

"You're not coming with me?"

"No. I want to meet this girl. There's a possibility we could adopt her child, and I want to talk to her today. I don't want to miss this opportunity. I don't want *us* to miss this opportunity."

Frustration creased his brow. "Fine. You stay. I'll get your suitcase from the car."

When he turned to go, she clasped his arm. "You *do* still want to adopt, don't you?"

"I want a child, Carrie. That doesn't mean I want a girl from the streets living here with us to accomplish that."

When Carrie released her husband's arm, he strode away.

Why had she said what she had? Why couldn't she let the meeting wait until Friday?

Because she felt as if a gulf was widening between her and Brian and if she didn't do something quickly, the distance between them could become permanent.

The instant Carrie laid eyes on Lisa Sanders a few hours later, she thought about catching the next flight to San Francisco and spending the day as she'd first intended. After introducing them to each other, Trina had left them alone.

Lisa was sitting in a chair in front of Trina's desk. Her hair was short and spiky, half red and half blond. Three earrings decorated both ears. There was a peace sign tattooed on her right wrist and an upside-down mermaid on her left arm. An oversized green T-shirt covered her belly and drooped over her jeans. Her pretty heart-shaped face was marred by green eyeshadow and purple lipstick. Carrie had spotted defiance in her big green eyes as soon as she'd walked into Trina's office.

Carrie knew what it felt like to be alone and lost and adrift without an anchor. She saw Lisa studying everything about her from her hair to her shoes. All she could do with this teenager was to be herself and hope it was enough.

Sitting across from Lisa in a matching chair, she opened conversation with, "I understand you're looking for a couple to adopt your baby."

The teenager's eyes widened as if she hadn't expected Carrie to be so forthright. Out of the blue she commented, "You're pretty. You used to be a model?"

From everything in her and Brian's file, she hadn't expected Lisa to ask her about that. "I used to be."

"Were you a runway model?"

"At the beginning. Then I was offered a contract with Modern Woman Cosmetics."

"Were you on TV?"

"Yes, I was."

"Wow. You really made it, then. Why'd you stop?"

"I got married. We wanted to have a family and modeling didn't fit into that."

"Your husband made you stop?"

"No. It was my choice. I decided to be a supportive wife, instead of a famous model." She said it lightly, but she suddenly realized she'd given up a lot of her independence when she'd left her profession.

"I've always wanted to model," Lisa said wistfully. "But now…" She folded her hands over her belly.

Carrie hoped Lisa hadn't picked her and Brian to talk to and possibly adopt her baby simply because she was interested in Carrie's past as a model.

"After you have your baby, you can be anything you want."

"Don't try to snow me," Lisa snapped. "We both know a homeless, unwed mother isn't going to get very far in this world."

"Don't be so sure. And don't underestimate yourself."

Lisa gave Carrie's outfit another once-over. "You probably came from a family with plenty of money. What would you know?" she muttered.

After a few moments of debate with herself, Carrie decided to share some of her background. "My parents were on welfare when I was growing up. I know a lot about being poor, Lisa. So does my husband. I sort of fell into modeling. My mother sent my picture into a contest and my career began there. With Brian, he's worked hard to become successful and he's done it all on his own."

When a long silence stretched between them, Carrie asked, "How did you become homeless?"

"I thought you'd ask how I got pregnant." There was a wryness to Lisa's tone.

"I think we both know how you did that. I want to know what brought you here and why you want to give up your baby."

Lisa stood, rubbed the small of her back, went to the window and looked out into the cloudy Portland winter. A stiff January wind was blowing the branches of maples and alders on the hospital complex.

In a monotone, she explained, "My parents were killed in an accident a few years ago. The only family I had left was Aunt Edna. She lived in Seattle and that's where they sent me."

"You were from Portland?"

"Yeah. I grew up here, but I couldn't stay. Our house was sold and they gave the money to my aunt to take care of me. Only she didn't. All she cared about were her soap operas. She went to bed at nine o'clock every night and thought I should get up with her at six in the morning. I hated living there. That's why I spent so much time with Thad. I thought he was cool. I thought he cared about me—"

Her voice broke off and Carrie felt so sorry for her.

Lisa composed herself and said bitterly, "He cared about one thing. That's all that was ever on his mind. I thought it meant he loved me. Love didn't have anything to do with it."

"I'm sure he must have cared—"

Lisa cut her off. "He cared so much, he told me he'd never admit to being the father. He said he'd tell everybody that I slept around. He said he had plans to get drafted by the NFL and no girl or baby was going to change that."

"So you ran?" Carrie guessed.

"I didn't run, I escaped. After graduation, I came back to Portland, got a room and a job waitressing. But I had morning sickness really bad and I couldn't work all my shifts. I couldn't pay for the room so they kicked me out. I learned how to get along," she insisted, her chin going up as she looked at Carrie now. "I'm eighteen and no one can tell me what to do."

"Do you want to give your baby up or do you feel you *have* to?"

The question seemed to perplex the teenager. "I don't want this kid. I don't want it to remind me how stupid I was. I don't want to have to take care of it twenty-four hours a day for the rest of its life."

"You might change your mind once you see your baby."

"I won't change my mind. I know I'll never get anywhere if I have to drag a kid along."

Lisa's words were tough, but Carrie didn't believe the girl was that tough. She just tried to make the world *think* she was.

"I want to be a mother more than I want anything," Carrie admitted.

"And I want to know my baby's going to a good home. Why didn't your husband come with you?"

"He had to fly to San Francisco today on business. I came to meet you."

Thinking about holding a baby in her arms, Carrie felt her heartbeats race with one another. Before she could catch the words, they soared out of her mouth. "How would you like to come live with us until you deliver? That way, you can decide if we're the couple you want to adopt your baby."

Now Carrie's stomach somersaulted. What was Brian going to say if Lisa accepted?

The grandfather clock in the foyer chimed six as Carrie added broccoli to the saucepan on the stove. Brian had insisted she have a housekeeper so she didn't have to worry about cleaning and cooking. They'd compromised and Verna came in three days a week, leaving casseroles on her days off, making sure the house was spic-and-span when she was there. Carrie supposed she'd fought against the idea of a housekeeper because she'd been used to taking care of a household and her three sisters while her mom worked. She missed it, actually. Now she couldn't help but smile as she started the preparation for cream of broccoli soup. She was going to fix salmon cakes to go with it.

Was she totally crazy bringing Lisa into their home?

She'd always had good instincts about people. On the outside, Lisa was defiant, sullen sometimes and looked a little wild. But Carrie's intuition told her that the girl was sensitive and looking for a place to belong, looking for a place for her baby to belong.

When the phone rang, Carrie froze midstride to the refrigerator. Her heart raced as she hurried to pick it up.

"Summers residence," she said, unable to keep the excitement from her voice because she suspected Brian was calling.

"Hi," he said in that deep tone that always curled her toes. "How did the interview go?"

She swallowed hard and jumped right in. "It went great. You've got to understand Lisa's background to understand *her,* and I think I do. And you can't let her appearance put you off. She has two-toned hair and tattoos. But she lost her parents, she's scared and she wants a home for her baby."

"I'm between meetings, Carrie. We can talk about it when I come home."

Only hesitating for a moment, she plunged ahead. "That's what I'm trying to tell you, Brian. I made the decision during the interview to invite Lisa to stay with us until she has her baby."

The complete silence that met Carrie's announcement wasn't broken even by cell phone static.

"You did what?"

The question was rhetorical, and she waited.

"How could you be so impulsive? How could you make a decision like this without consulting me? We don't know this girl, Carrie. We don't know who she is or where she's been. She's been living on the streets—" He stopped abruptly.

Sometimes Brian handled Carrie as if she were a piece of glass, and she wasn't sure why. He didn't know about the rape or the abortion or the counseling that had saved her life and her future. Yet he held back with her. He always seemed to hold back, and she guessed he was holding back angry words now.

He'd never seen how strong she could be. Maybe it was time to show him. "I know you believe my decision was impulsive. Maybe it was, but I'm going into this with my eyes open. If we can show Lisa we can be caring parents and that we'll be the best parents for her baby, we'll have a child. Isn't that more important than a little inconvenience?"

She heard his sigh, and his words were filled with concern. "I'm not worried about the inconvenience. I'm being cautious. This might not turn out the way you want, and you'll be hurt. This girl could change her mind about adoption or decide she'd rather place her child elsewhere."

"I know that. But Lisa will give me something worthwhile to do while you're away on business. Volunteer work is fine, but taking care of Lisa will be like taking care of my sisters. I've missed that."

His silence went long. Finally he responded, "I know you have. But the timing of this— For the next month or so I'll be on call. This land deal in Alaska is important. I think you've made a mistake, and you need to rectify it before this girl settles in."

"You're *always* on call, Brian, and all the deals are important. I'm used to that." She had never put her resignation into words before but now she did so. She was fighting for this chance to make their marriage strong again, and intuitively she knew Lisa and her baby were part of that. "I know we can make this work."

His voice was clipped when he replied, "I'll be flying home tonight instead of tomorrow. I should be there around eleven-thirty."

"Brian, I couldn't leave her in that shelter another night."

"We'll talk about it when I get home."

Yes, they would. Having Lisa in their home might not be easy, but inviting her to stay had been the right choice. Somehow Carrie would convince her husband of that.

A few hours later as Brian came in the door from the garage, Carrie was there waiting for him, hoping to ease him into an introduction to Lisa.

First, though, she smiled and asked, "Are you hungry?"

A flash of desire in Brian's eyes reminded her of the other night and the way they'd made love. It had been different somehow. She'd almost felt Brian wasn't holding back, that he'd let himself go and she'd responded to that. Yet afterward he'd withdrawn. Sometimes she felt as if she were doing a complicated dance with her husband, afraid she'd misstep and the rhythm would be broken forever.

Setting down his overnighter and his briefcase, he bent to her, letting his lips say his "hello," letting his kiss tell her he'd missed her.

Ending it, he straightened. "No. I'm not hungry. Dinner was elaborate." Picking up his luggage once more, he crossed the kitchen. "During the flight, I thought about what we should do. You've gotten us into a situation. Our only resort now is to put this girl in a hotel suite—"

"No! That's not the answer. Especially since you haven't even met her."

Brian stopped and turned.

"Lisa's blood pressure is a bit elevated," she hurried

on. "She needs someone to look after her. I can do that here. Brian, please. The easy course isn't always the best one. Besides, if she doesn't live with us, why would she want to choose us? Why would she want to let *us* adopt her baby?"

It was obvious Brian was struggling with all of it. He didn't want his life disrupted, especially not by a stranger off the streets. But he did want a child. "Where is she?" he asked.

"In the family room. I told her to make herself comfortable. She's been watching TV."

He finally said, "All right. I'll meet her." Striding to the foyer, he deposited his luggage by the staircase.

When Carrie hurried after him, she warned in a low voice, "Don't make a first impression just from her appearance. She's—"

Before Carrie could finish her sentence, he'd already headed for the family room. There he stopped and took in the scene with a frown.

It had been a long day, and Brian saw it was going to get much longer. Carrie had never done anything like this before—made a decision without consulting him. He wondered what was at the bottom of it now. Did she want a baby that badly?

He stared at Lisa Sanders in stunned amazement. Yes, Carrie had told him she had two-toned hair and tattoos. But she hadn't told him one tattoo was an upside-down mermaid that started at Lisa's elbow and disappeared under her T-shirt sleeve, and that the teenager's hair wasn't only two-toned, it was spiked and sticking out at all angles. Three earrings dangled from both ears and her lipstick was purple!

Restraining the desire to tell Lisa to take her sneakered feet off the mahogany coffee table and change the loud music-video station on the TV to something quieter, he counted to ten. So many questions clicked through his head as he felt anger rise at Carrie for putting them in this position.

However, when he caught the worried expression on his wife's face, he kept his tone as casual as he could. "You must be Lisa." His gut told him nothing about having this teenager around would be easy.

As she finished eating a banana, she proved his instincts right when she defiantly asked, "Why must I be Lisa? Because I'm pregnant or because my hair is more than one color?" She cast a defiant glance at Carrie. "What did you tell him about me?"

The teenager didn't seem to ruffle Carrie as his wife replied, "I told him you've lost your parents and you have nowhere to go."

"My wife told me very little," Brian said. "I think she wanted me to meet you and form my own conclusions. Do you think you could turn down the sound on the TV?"

Lisa gave him a look that said this whole interview was an imposition.

But he wasn't going to let her make him feel uncomfortable in his own house. "I think we should talk *if* you're going to stay here."

With that she took her feet from the coffee table, flipped a banana peel into the waste can next to the sofa and switched off the TV. "If you don't want me here, you'd better say so now."

"I don't know you," he admitted freely. "Carrie made the decision to ask you to stay here without talking to me first."

"She has to check with you on everything?"

"We're married, Lisa. Married couples discuss major decisions. This is one of those, especially if you decide to let us adopt your baby."

Lisa focused her attention on Carrie. "Were you afraid he'd say no if you asked him?"

After a glance at him Carrie answered, "After I met you, I decided we could both benefit from this arrangement. You need a roof over your head, and we want to adopt."

"And he could put up with anything for a month?"

"Something like that," Carrie confessed with a small smile to lighten the atmosphere.

Some of the tension seemed to leave Lisa's shoulders, although Brian didn't feel any more at ease. Now she addressed him again. "Do you want a baby as much as Carrie does?"

"We want a family," he said.

"You want a *baby*," Lisa pressed.

"Yes." Seeing Lisa's large belly brought home the reality that he could be a father much sooner than he'd expected.

Carrie sat beside Lisa on the sofa. "I know this is overwhelming, and I know you don't feel at home here yet—"

Sliding to the edge of the sofa cushion, Lisa pushed herself up to her feet. "At home? I shouldn't even think about feeling at home. Even if this does work out, I'll be gone in a month. Not much different from the shelter, though it *is* a lot better furnished." She looked squarely at Brian. "So am I staying or leaving?"

He hated being pushed into a corner, and it was reflexive for him to fight to get out. Yet he had to be careful he didn't shatter their dreams because he was angry at Carrie. Looking at his wife now, he could see she was worried. About Lisa? About his reaction?

His answer for Lisa came quickly. "You can stay."

To his surprise, he didn't see relief on her face, or gratitude. Passing by him, the teenager stopped at the doorway to the living room, turned and threw over her shoulder, "If I decide not to give you the baby, you'll throw me out, won't you?"

Carrie rose to her feet. After a look at Brian, she replied softly, "No. You need a place to stay until your baby is born. No matter what happens, that won't change."

Lisa looked at Brian. "Does that go for you, too?"

Whatever had gotten into Carrie, this was apparently important to her. "My wife made you a promise. I'll abide by that."

If Lisa felt thankful at his words, she didn't show it. Instead she headed for the guest bedroom next to his study.

After her footsteps had faded away, Brian turned to Carrie. "She's going to be more than you bargained for."

"She's scared. Can't you see that?"

"No, I can't. But then she didn't give me the opportunity to find out much about her. I have lots of questions, Carrie. What kind of baby will we be adopting? What kind of life has she led since she's been on the streets? Is she taking drugs? Who's the father? Does she even know?"

Carrie held up a hand to stop the barrage. "She knows who the father is. The caseworker has already contacted him and he's given up his parental rights. There's no evidence Lisa has taken drugs. If I can get to know her better, maybe she'll tell me more. The bottom line is, Brian, if she gives us this child can we love him or her, no matter what, the same as we would our own child?"

"You're asking a hell of a lot, Carrie. We could have tried in vitro again. A surrogate might even be better than this. At least she'd be screened and the child would be half mine."

"We tried in vitro twice and it didn't work. I can't go through that again, Brian—the waiting, the hoping. And as far as a surrogate goes, can you only father a child that was made with your sperm? Is that what you're saying?"

Rubbing the back of his neck, he shook his head. "No, that's not what I'm saying. There are so many unknown factors here. You made an impulsive decision based on emotion!"

"I made a decision because we want to be parents. It isn't only Lisa's baby. I think she has the attitude she does because she thinks we're trying to use her, that we aren't going to really care about *her*. During our interview today, I began caring about her. That's why I asked her to stay here."

The truth was, he felt ambushed. He felt as if Carrie had crossed some line that defined them as a couple by making this decision on her own. He knew he hadn't completely dealt with the disappointment of not raising a child that he and Carrie had created together.

"If you want to give this girl a home for now, we'll do that. As far as the baby goes, we don't have to commit to this child until Lisa commits to us. By that time, maybe we'll have more answers. I know you want her to like us. I know you want her to see us as the best couple to raise her baby. But we can't pretend to be what we're not, either."

"Don't you think we do pretend sometimes?" Carrie asked quietly.

"Pretend what?"

"Pretend to be happier than we are—at parties, with other couples, even sometimes when we're alone."

Her words were as shocking as a plunge into ice water. "Aren't you happy?"

"I am, but… Since we've been trying to have a baby, ever since we've had trouble trying to have a baby, things have changed between us. Don't you feel that?"

Changed? He hadn't felt anything change until today. After a moment's consideration, he responded, "I think we've both been on a roller-coaster and that's taken its toll."

"We're still on the roller-coaster."

His wife had never looked so troubled. Even as frustrated as he was with her at this moment, her beauty—inside and out—always got to him. "I guess we are. Somehow we'll have to figure out how to survive the hills and dips together. Isn't that what marriage is all about?"

"Yes, it's just—" Giving him a slight smile she shook her head. "Never mind. I'm going to see if Lisa needs anything."

Before Carrie could leave the room, Brian clasped her hand.

She stopped and faced him.

"I want you to be happy, Carrie. I want this all to work out."

"I do, too. I'm afraid of what will happen to us if it doesn't."

And then his wife slipped from his grasp.

Brian wished he could read her mind. This adoption obviously meant everything to her. He wondered if he truly knew the reason why.

Three

On Saturday night when Brian entered the kitchen looking for Carrie, he felt a nerve in his jaw work. He immediately caught sight of her speaking to the caterer. She wore a beaded, royal-blue dress with long sleeves and a demure neckline, and he reluctantly admitted his wife had never looked more beautiful. With her hair caught at the nape of her neck in a sleek chignon, a few wavy tendrils framed her face. She'd clasped around her neck a sapphire necklace he'd given her for Christmas, and she looked...like a princess. All she needed was the tiara.

All *he* needed was a cold shower!

Setting aside the impulse to pull the pins from her hair and mess up her lipstick, he replaced desire with restraint. He didn't want to need her right now. He was still angry she'd changed the whole dynamic of their lives by inviting Lisa to live with them. They hadn't made love since before Lisa had arrived. For the past few nights, there had seemed to be an impenetrable fence down the center of their bed.

When Carrie saw him, she finished her consultation with the caterer and crossed to him.

"You're beautiful tonight." He couldn't help complimenting her in spite of the tension between them.

She looked surprised for a moment. "You're looking quite handsome yourself."

Just standing here with Carrie now, looking at her, breathing in the classic scent of her perfume, he realized his body was completely aroused. He put the brakes on his libido. "Is everything ready?"

"Just about."

"Where's Lisa?"

Carrie looked worried. "She spent most of the day in her room. I made her soup and a salad for lunch."

After a glance at the caterer, Brian took Carrie by the elbow and shepherded her into the short hallway that led to the garage. "You're headed for disappointment if you expect anything from that girl. She's a rebellious teenager. Her story tells you that. She's not a stray puppy you can bring into the house, feed and pamper and who will love you unconditionally. You're going to get hurt if you want more from her than a thank-you when she leaves. I don't even know if she'll give you that." As far as he was concerned, Carrie's soft heart had to be protected, and she needed to see the reality of the situation.

But her response told him she didn't. "Maybe I'm more hopeful than you are. Maybe I'm hoping to form a bond with her so she can trust me. She's been hurt, Brian, by her parents' death, by her boyfriend walking away, by her aunt's attitude, which seemed to tell her she was a bother."

"You can't perform miracles in a month." Carrie had never before been quite so determined, quite so adamant that she could make a difference.

When Carrie took a step closer to him, there was so much longing in her dark-brown eyes, he couldn't look away. She touched his set jaw with a caressing stroke that made fireworks shoot through his veins.

"Maybe I can't perform miracles," she murmured, "but I need to try."

Her soft words crumbled his restraint. He couldn't help but reach out and smooth his hand along the side of Carrie's face. Her eyes became a deeper brown, and her lips parted ever so slightly. She always responded to his touch and he to hers. Drawing her to him, his lips seared hers. He held on to the passion, kept the kiss short but couldn't resist stroking her tongue with his. Then he reluctantly released her and stepped away, hungry for her. That hunger never diminished. Yet he kept it in check, and he wasn't sure why.

The doorbell rang and they could hear it even in the corridor outside of the laundry room.

Breaking eye contact, Carrie glanced under her sleeve at a department-store watch that fit her wrist like a bracelet. It had been a gift from her sisters last Christmas. He could buy her a diamond watch and had offered to, but she preferred wearing this one. He'd realized long ago sentiment meant more to Carrie than quality or monetary value. He was afraid sentiment where Lisa was concerned would hurt them both.

"We have to greet our guests." She put her fingers to her lips. "I'll stop in the powder room first."

When she conjured up a smile, he fought the urge to kiss her all over again.

The doorbell rang once more, and Brian went to the foyer. There were two couples there—the O'Briens and the Hammonds—as well as Derrick Dennehy, who'd obviously come without his wife. That was peculiar since he'd spoken to Derrick the day before yesterday and the lawyer had assured Brian they'd both be there. Maybe Jackie had picked up the flu bug that was going around.

As Carrie joined them and guided the O'Briens and the Hammonds into the living room where hors d'oeuvres were waiting, Derrick held back and grabbed Brian's arm. After the maid had gone to the kitchen, he said, "Jackie couldn't make it tonight."

Something in Derrick's voice warned Brian it wasn't a simple flu bug that had kept his wife away.

Adjusting his striped silk tie, Derrick looked uncomfortable. "She moved out yesterday and it looks as if we'll be getting a divorce. I had no idea this was coming. It came out of the blue."

The same age as Brian—in their midthirties—Derrick and Jackie had been married after their college graduation.

"Out of the blue?"

Derrick shook his head in exasperation. "You'd think I'd know a woman after living with her for twelve years. But then she said *that* was the problem. She maintains I haven't really been living with her all these years. I've been spending too many nights in my office, too many weekends out of town drumming up more business so she could drive that fancy new Italian sports car. Now she tells me she's met someone who makes her the center of his world. I don't know how he can do that and work, too!"

Abruptly Derrick shook his head. "I didn't mean to go into all that. You're the first person I've told."

"I'm sorry, Derrick. Is there anything I can do?"

"Yes. Put together this deal in Alaska. It will give me something else to think about. The contracts to develop it would keep me busy for the next few months."

As an attorney, Derrick took care of much of the legal work that came up with the projects Brian coordinated. "I'll see what I can do."

Carrie raised questioning eyes to Brian as he and Derrick entered the living room. Brian gave a slight shake of his head, and when neither he nor Derrick explained why Jackie wasn't present, Carrie understood she should stay away from that topic.

It wasn't until Ted Hammond, Rob O'Brien and Derrick were engaged in business conversation and Ted and Rob's wives had escaped to freshen up in the powder room, that Brian took Carrie aside out of earshot of everyone to explain, "Jackie left Derrick."

Carrie was shocked. "You're not serious."

"He never saw it coming. She found someone else." To Brian, that was what it boiled down to.

Because Carrie looked pensive, Brian asked, "Did you know? Did she say anything to you?" The circle of women who ran the foundation boards Carrie served on included Jackie.

"When I had lunch with her before Christmas, she'd been unusually quiet. In the past she's mentioned that she's been lonely and Derrick is never home."

"Well, he wasn't seeing other women. He was working."

Brian knew his tone was defensive, but he was identifying with Derrick. He added, "She belonged to as many committees as you do. I don't understand how she could be lonely."

"Committees and volunteer work are not the same thing as intimate time with a spouse."

Intimate time. Time in bed when a husband and wife coupled? Or was Carrie talking about conversations over dinner for two, an impromptu visit to the zoo, a walk in the rain? They hadn't done any of those for a long time.

Peggy O'Brien and Carla Hammond were laughing as they came into the foyer. Peggy patted Carrie's shoulder. "My, my, my. You two look much too serious. Is there a problem?"

Brian could see his wife consciously relax and find a smile for her guests. Once, she'd told him she'd had training in relaxation techniques. He supposed that had something to do with learning to pose for the camera.

Now he could almost believe she wasn't still thinking about their conversation as she said to Peggy, "Dinner will be ready any minute. You can have your choice of wines to go with the seafood Newburgh and prime rib. The server will explain the merits of each. Let's gather everyone and go into the dining room."

Brian marveled at Carrie's ease in turning the conversation to their guests. His wife definitely had tact. Maybe that came from having to referee three sisters vying for her parents' attention.

However, although Carrie had changed the subject smoothly, it hadn't left Brian's mind—neither Derrick's situation nor his wife's comments.

Though Derrick was quieter than normal, conversation flowed smoothly over dinner. As usual the women spoke of charities, theater selections for the year, and new worthwhile causes. The men always turned to business. After German chocolate cake had been served, Rob focused his attention on Brian.

"I think it's time we talk about what's really on our minds. How are the Alaskan negotiations going?" Rob was an investment banker who worked closely with Brian.

"A bit touchy," Brian admitted. "But I don't see any major problems. I'm going to have to fly up there soon to do some reassuring in person."

"I expected that," Ted said. "The environment is important to them." Ted worked for Brian, chasing down leads on real estate.

After Ted ate the last bite of his chocolate cake with gusto and took a sip of black coffee, he asked, "Are you interested in investing in more land in Hawaii? I've got wind of an entrepreneur who's thinking about selling. You and Carrie could take a week, fly over there and see what it's like. Danny Crosby was pleased with the deal you put together for him. Maybe he'd spread the word."

Danny Crosby, the son of one of the richest families in Portland, had bought his own island and Brian had been instrumental in that. Danny was a man who had suffered the tragedies of his family deeply, and Brian had become friends with him through the man's search for the right reclusive property. "Danny Crosby keeps to himself on his island."

"But if he put the word out…" Ted prompted.

"I'm not going to take advantage of him or his family's reputation. I *will* ask him if I can use him as a reference, though."

"That in itself would be a plus," Rob agreed. "The

Crosby name has always carried weight, as much as the Logans'. By the way, I heard the Logans have donated even more money to Children's Connection. Their coffers seem to be bottomless."

The Logans were as rich as the Crosbys. Their involvement with the Children's Connection adoption agency and fertility clinic went back years. Danny Crosby and Robbie Logan had been best friends as kids. But when six-year-old Robbie had been kidnapped from the Crosbys' yard and Sheila Crosby, Danny's mother, had been blamed, a feud had developed between the two families. Recovery for the Logans over the loss of their son had been slow, but they poured their passion and time into the adoption agency and the fertility clinic and gone on as best they could. He wasn't sure the Crosbys would ever recover.

Addressing Carrie, Ted asked, "So how does a trip to Hawaii sound?"

Carrie's gaze met Brian's. "This isn't a good time for me to get away."

Before Ted could question her, loud music erupted from down the hall. Very loud music. All of their guests looked startled.

"What's that?" Derrick asked. "Are you having a rap concert in your backyard?"

Suddenly Lisa with her geometrically designed red-and-blond hair—now half spiked, half flat—appeared in a T-shirt that looked as if it should be in a trash bin. Her jeans were tattered, too.

Carrie was out of her chair in a second, and Brian felt himself rising to his feet.

"I got hungry," the teen mumbled, glancing around at everybody.

"I'm glad," Carrie said with a smile, putting her arm around Lisa. Without hesitation, she said to the group at the table, "This is Lisa Sanders. She's staying with us for a while. Lisa, meet Mr. and Mrs. Hammond, Mr. and Mrs. O'Brien, and Mr. Dennehy."

Brian suspected his guests were still trying to recover from the shock of Lisa's appearance.

Carrie excused herself and suggested to Lisa, "Come into the kitchen with me and I'll get you a platter."

As soon as his wife and Lisa disappeared, all eyes were on Brian. "Lisa's thinking about giving up her baby for adoption, and we might adopt."

"How long have you been planning this?" Peggy asked, speaking loud enough to be heard over the music.

"Not long. Lisa came to stay a few days ago."

Carla leaned back in her chair and pushed her plate away with two bites of cake still on it. "You and Carrie tried in vitro, didn't you?"

Brian didn't like talking about his personal life this way, but he supposed Carrie had confided in these women. "Yes, we did."

Peggy shook her head. "It's a shame you have to resort to this."

Although those had been Brian's thoughts, he bristled. "Like all children, Lisa's baby deserves a good home. Carrie and I can provide that." Deciding to end the conversation right there, he rose to his feet. "I'll see what's keeping Carrie."

As soon as he stepped into the kitchen, he was aware the caterer wasn't making a platter for Lisa at all but stowing away the remains of the dinner. Carrie, however, was creating a thick sandwich while Lisa looked on.

"Did we eat all the prime rib?" he asked, trying to keep his voice tempered.

"Lisa just wanted something more simple."

Lisa's music still blared loudly into the whole house. "If you don't mind, Lisa, I'm going to turn down the music."

"I do mind. I'm listening to it."

His patience wore thin. "Unfortunately, so are our guests. They're trying to have a conversation."

Lisa's face grew defiant. "I suppose it would be better for you if I hadn't come out at all. I saw the way they looked at me."

Carrie dropped the butter knife she'd been using, and Lisa stooped to pick it up. When she tried to straighten, she wobbled.

Brian saw her losing her balance and he went to her quickly, helping her. "What's wrong?"

"Just felt dizzy." Her face had flushed and Brian didn't like that.

"When did you last eat?" he asked.

"Around noon." Her voice trailed off as she sagged against him.

Without thinking about it twice, he lifted her into his arms. "I'm taking her to her room."

Looking scared, Lisa held on tightly. Suddenly Brian didn't see the two-colored hair, the earrings, the tattoos. He saw a young girl whose world was swirling around her and she couldn't seem to stop it.

The guest bedroom on the first floor was decorated in yellow and white and pink. A hand-quilted comforter in those colors lay across the bed while a white dust ruffle peeked out from under it. The yellow armchair in the corner of the room was a comfortable one and Brian could see that was where Lisa had apparently spent most of her time, since there was a romance novel and a few magazines spread around it. The CD player was still blaring and Carrie went to it, switching it off. She'd managed to grab the sandwich and a glass of milk.

Now as Brian laid Lisa on the bed, Carrie set the food on the nightstand and crouched down beside the teenager.

"Do you have a headache?" she asked as she pulled up Lisa's jeans—to check her ankles for swelling, Brian guessed.

"No headache. Just a little dizzy." At the dresser, Carrie opened one of the drawers and pulled out a blood pressure monitor. With a sideways glance at him, she said, "I bought it yesterday. Since Lisa was taken to the emergency room because her blood pressure was too high, I thought we'd better keep track of it."

After she put the cuff around Lisa's arm, she waited for the digital readout. A short time later the machine beeped. "It's slightly elevated. I think you'd better rest for the evening."

"I'm so bored," Lisa groaned. "I've been reading and looking at magazines since I've been here. That's the only CD I've kept and I'm tired of it. This baby is ruining my life!"

Brian sat down on the bed beside Lisa. "I don't think it's the baby who's ruining your life. Circumstances are, and maybe a few wrong decisions on your part."

Lisa glared at him. "You think you have all the right answers."

Making an effort not to let her get to him, he replied,

"There are a lot of problems to be solved here. You can't do it all instantly or even overnight. If you want help, we'll guide you in the right direction. You need to be thinking about what you want to do after your baby's born. If you give it up for adoption—"

"You bet I'm giving it up for adoption. I don't want to take care of it all day and all night. I want—"

Tears came into her eyes, and Brian actually felt sorry for her. Maybe this was how Carrie had felt toward the teenager since their first meeting.

"What do you want?" he asked in a low voice.

"What I want can never happen. I want my parents back. I want my body back."

Carrie spoke softly from the other side of the bed. "I'm sorry about your parents, Lisa. I can only imagine how you feel—absolutely alone with no one to hold on to. But you don't have to be alone now. We want to help."

There was a slight rap on the door, and Peggy stepped inside. "Is there something wrong? Is there anything we can do?"

Brian suspected Peggy didn't want anything to do as much as she wanted to see what was going on. She was the typical social butterfly and he often doubted her sincerity. "We have everything under control. Carrie and I will be out in a couple of minutes. Tell Rob to help himself to some of that cognac on the buffet."

"The caterer just set out divine liqueurs. We didn't want to start without you."

"Go right ahead. We'll join you shortly."

With a last look at Lisa, Peggy left the room, high heels clicking on the hardwood floor.

After Carrie stood, she picked up the sandwich on the

nightstand and offered it to Lisa. "You've got to eat regular meals, too. It will help. I'll stay here and keep you company while Brian goes back to our guests."

That wasn't an option Brian preferred. "I can bring a TV in here from the guest room upstairs. Then you won't have to stay."

Carrie's dark eyes met his. "The TV's a good idea. But I want to make sure Lisa's over her dizziness. I'm sure everyone will understand."

He wasn't sure they *would* understand. There was a time when Carrie wouldn't have considered bailing out of one of his social functions. "Can I talk to you in the hall for a minute?"

Lisa was eating the sandwich and Carrie told her, "I'll be right back."

Brian moved away from the door and kept his voice low. "She's fine, Carrie. I'll bring down the TV and you can look in on her every once in a while."

"We made a mistake by not including her in the dinner party."

"The dinner party is a business function. Why would we include her?"

"Because she's alone and she's looking for a place to belong."

"*You* belong with our guests," he said, a firmness shading his voice.

"They're *your* guests, Brian. This is *your* business function. After the cordials, Peggy and Carla will talk about fashion shows while you, Derrick, Ted and Rob plan how you can make your next million. I don't think my absence from that discussion is going to be a great loss."

There was a fire in Carrie when she became protective of Lisa. She'd never spoken to him this way before. Part of him was annoyed that she wasn't living up to her part of her commitment as his wife. Yet another part of him was fascinated by the independent woman she'd apparently kept hidden inside. The huge question was why.

"Tell me something, Carrie. Do you really want to spend time with Lisa? Or do you just want to escape chitchat with the O'Briens and Hammonds?"

After only a moment's hesitation, Carrie spoke softly. "If Lisa lets us adopt her child, in a way she'll become family. It's important for me to get to know her. It's important for her to feel that she's *not* a stray we just dragged in. Can't you see that? Can't you see that family has to come before business?"

What he saw was that Carrie was changing. With adopting a baby, their lives would change. He'd never had to be flexible. Since he was a kid, he'd been determined to make something of himself as his father hadn't. He'd set his course and stayed on it. Right was right, wrong was wrong and success made a man's life worthwhile. Even when Carrie had entered the picture, his life hadn't taken any radical turns. She'd fit in. She'd gone along. He was beginning to realize their marriage had always been about what *he* wanted, not what Carrie wanted. Is that why she'd always held back a part of herself? Was she afraid to let her independence and self-assurance emerge in the wake of his more substantial goals?

Figuring all of that into the equation, he said, "I'll make your excuses. But I'm also going to go upstairs and get that TV. If Lisa decides to turn silent on you, she can watch it and you can come back out and say good-night. Fair enough?"

"Fair enough," Carrie murmured.

When Brian headed for the stairs, he felt his wife's gaze on him and he realized he'd give that million dollars Carrie had mentioned to know exactly what she was thinking.

Early the next morning, Brian slipped out of bed, pulled on jogging shorts and went to the exercise room in the basement to work out. Last night, Carrie had never returned to their guests. She'd still been in Lisa's room when he'd bid them good-night. Afterward, he'd worked in his office until he'd heard her exit the teenager's room. When they'd gone up to bed together, there had been a strain between them and they'd stayed on separate sides of the bed. He hadn't reached for her and she hadn't turned to him. He wasn't sure what was happening. He just knew something was.

He thought about what Derrick had said. *It came out of the blue.* Maybe that wasn't so unusual. Maybe husbands and wives never did really know what the other was thinking.

After an extralong workout on the Nautilus and a one-sided match with the punching bag, Brian showered downstairs and dressed in sweats he kept there. When he went up to the kitchen, Carrie was beating eggs with a whisk.

"Would you like scrambled eggs?" she asked. "Lisa isn't up, but I'm hoping when she smells the bacon and toast, she'll join us."

Carrie hadn't dressed yet. She wore an ice-blue silk robe over a matching nightgown. As always, she looked feminine and elegant, so beautiful his chest hurt just looking at her.

"Breakfast for two would be nice, too," he offered, tired of the discord between them.

When Carrie's gaze met his, she sighed. "I didn't mean to let you down last night. But Lisa and I began talking and I thought that was more important. She's afraid, Brian. Afraid of the pain of labor and delivery, afraid of what's going to happen afterward, afraid she's never going to be able to afford an apartment or get a job."

He didn't want this conversation to be about Lisa but rather about them. Throughout the night he'd tossed and turned over all of it. "I understand why you want to help Lisa. You want her baby."

"It's more than that! I'm not just trying to win her over. I care about her."

He could see that she did and wondered how she could care so easily. "All right, you care. I just don't want you to get hurt while you're caring."

"This is one time when I'm going to take the risk and maybe you'll have to, too."

Although he tolerated risks every day he did business, he'd never had to tolerate them in his personal life. "Do you have something particular in mind?"

She flushed. "Yes. I'm taking Lisa to an obstetrician tomorrow afternoon. Dr. Grieb will probably do a sonogram. I thought maybe you'd like to come along and see the baby we might be adopting."

He knew exactly what Carrie was doing. She wanted to make this baby a reality. *Their* reality. "What time is the appointment?"

"Three o'clock."

He knew his appointments tomorrow were stacked back to back because of being out of town last week. "I'll do my best to clear my calendar, and I'll try to meet you there."

This appointment was important to Carrie, and he suddenly understood how it might be terrifically important to him, too.

Four

Carrie and Lisa had just taken seats in the obstetrician's office when Carrie's cell phone buzzed. Smiling at Lisa, she said, "I'll be right back," and went around the corner from the reception area where the coat closet was located.

"Hello?" She recognized the number on her caller ID as the exchange of the hospital.

"Carrie? It's Nancy. Can you talk?"

Nancy Allen was one of the nicest people Carrie knew. Always considerate, she genuinely cared about others, especially children. Carrie had discovered she was the nurse who had called the caseworker from Children's Connection to help Lisa when the teenager had been brought into the E.R.

"Hi, Nancy. What's up?"

"I know you took Lisa Sanders home with you and you probably have your hands full. But I wondered if you're busy tomorrow morning? Sherry Winslow, who's supposed to read to kids in Peds, caught a flu bug and can't come. Are you available?"

Somehow Nancy always heard about everything. Lots of people had seen Lisa leave the adoption agency with Carrie. "I'm at the obstetrician's office with Lisa now. Let me see how her checkup goes. If everything's okay, I'll be glad to read to the kids tomorrow."

"That would be great. How's Lisa doing?"

"As well as can be expected, I guess. I've spent some time with her. She's really missing her parents and needs a listening ear to help her through this."

"Is she getting along okay with Brian?" Nancy asked.

Carrie chose her words carefully. "Brian's not sure yet what to make of Lisa. And Lisa isn't too sure what to make of Brian."

"If you're acting as a buffer, I'm sure everything will be fine. Has she made a decision yet about letting you adopt the baby?"

"No, but she doesn't really know us yet."

"You and Brian are good people. She'll figure that out soon."

All of Carrie's hopes were pinned on Lisa, though she knew she couldn't rush the teenager's decision. "Do you want me to leave a message for you at the E.R.?" she asked, knowing Nancy was probably on break and didn't have much time to talk.

"My cell phone's in my locker. You can just leave a message on my voice mail. Do you have the number?"

"Yes."

"Good. I'll retrieve the message at lunch."

"Are you still having lunches with Everett?" Carrie asked in a teasing tone.

"Whenever he's not too busy and our schedules co-incide. I *am* meeting him today. He's such a complicated man. I have trouble understanding him sometimes, but I do like him."

"Maybe a little more than 'like'?" Carrie asked kindly.

"Maybe a lot more than 'like.'"

At that moment, the receptionist in the waiting room called Lisa's name. "I've got to go. The doctor's ready for Lisa. I'll talk to you later."

After Carrie disconnected, thoughts of Nancy led to thoughts of Everett again and his offer of help with a private adoption. She'd intended to ask Nancy about Everett's connections but had forgotten. Next time they didn't have a hurried conversation, maybe Carrie could find out more. If this adoption with Lisa fell through, she and Brian might want to consider Everett's suggestion.

As Carrie followed Lisa and the nurse to an examination room, she was disappointed Brian hadn't arrived yet. Maybe he was backing away altogether from the idea of adopting Lisa's child.

Lisa asked Carrie to stay with her while the doctor examined her. As the nurse readied Lisa for the sonogram, Carrie gave her an encouraging smile. Finally the doctor took the wand in hand.

There was a soft rap on the door. A nurse peeked her head inside. "Mr. Summers is here. He said Lisa invited him to see the sonogram."

Carrie knew the caseworker had made the doctor aware of Lisa's situation and the possibility that Carrie and Brian might become this baby's parents.

Lisa raised herself up on her elbows. "He can come in and watch with Carrie."

As Brian stepped into the room, he looked uncomfortable. The doctor nodded to him and arranged the sheet so she was wielding the wand behind it. "If you sit over there with your wife, you can watch the monitor," Dr. Grieb suggested.

As Brian sat beside her, Carrie felt his shoulder brush hers. When she glanced at him, she saw his hair was ruffled from the wind. His tie, perfectly knotted, was slightly off-center, though his navy suit coat fit his shoulders impeccably and made them look even broader.

"I thought maybe you couldn't clear your schedule."

"My last appointment ran late. I was hoping I would get here in time."

"I'm glad you did."

"Here we go," the doctor announced. "Keep your eyes on the monitor, and I'll try to explain as we go."

Carrie's gaze was glued to the screen. In a few moments she made out the shape of the baby. "Look!" she exclaimed, reaching for Brian's hand. "Isn't that amazing?"

"Do you want to know the sex?" the doctor asked with a smile.

Lisa nodded.

"You're going to have a boy," Dr. Grieb said, grinning.

When Carrie stole another glance at her husband, he was watching the screen with as much focus as she'd ever seen on his face. A boy. A son. Could Brian imagine that as she could?

The picture changed a little and Carrie asked, "Is he sucking his thumb?"

"It looks that way," the doctor agreed.

Brian leaned close to Carrie and her gaze met his. She saw something in his darkening eyes that thrilled her and told her he was as touched by this preview as she was.

"I think an adoption is going to work," he said in a low voice.

"I think so, too." When Brian extended his arm around Carrie's shoulders, he pulled her to him for a few moments then released her.

A short time later when the doctor finished with the wand and wiped the gel from Lisa's tummy, Brian and Carrie stood.

"We'll wait outside until you're dressed," Carrie assured the teenager.

Lisa's expression was more serious than Carrie ever had seen it as she nodded.

A short time later, when Lisa entered the reception room, Brian had just written out a check for the doctor's services and the receptionist handed him a receipt. Watching all of it with a grave expression, Lisa finally asked, "Are you going back to work?"

He looked surprised at her question. "Yes, I am. Why?"

"I'd like to talk to you and Carrie."

He checked his watch. "I'll follow you home."

As Carrie drove, there was silence in her car. Carrie wondered if seeing the baby on the monitor had awakened Lisa's motherly instincts. Maybe she'd changed her mind about giving the baby up. A knot tightened in Carrie's stomach.

What was Brian feeling about all of this? Was he worried, too, that Lisa would want to keep her baby? He was so good at controlling his emotions. He'd once told Carrie she'd make a terrible poker player because she didn't know how to bluff. She'd never played poker with Brian, but she suspected he'd be very good at it.

When Brian came in, Lisa was sitting in the living room and Carrie was trying not to pace.

"Is everything all right?" he asked the teenager. "With your health? With the baby?"

"The doctor said I'm doing okay. I'm supposed to rest when I'm tired and take my blood pressure if I feel dizzy. I told her Carrie had one of those cuffs. I don't really want to talk to you about all that. It's the baby."

"Go on," Brian encouraged her.

Carrie could see he was truly worried.

Lisa looked down at her tummy under the huge T-shirt. "I guess I really didn't see this kid as real before today, even though I look like this." She tried to give both of them a little smile. "But when I saw that sonogram—"

She stopped and looked at Carrie with moist eyes. "I knew I had to do something. I knew I had to make a decision. About the two of you, I mean."

Carrie felt as if her whole life, her whole marriage, depended on what Lisa was going to say next. Sitting down beside her, she waited, her heart pounding.

"You two really want a baby, I can tell. And I can see from all this—" she waved at the furniture and the draperies in the living room "—that you can give this kid a good life, every possible advantage. I picked you out of a whole lot of other people for a bunch of reasons. I wanted to see if you matched up to what I read. I think you do. So if you want to adopt this baby after it's born, you can."

Brian looked over at Carrie then back at Lisa. "Are you sure you want to make this decision so quickly? You've known us less than a week."

"I'm sure." Pushing herself to her feet, she gave both of them a weak smile. "I'm tired. I'm going to my room to rest now."

Before Lisa could move toward her room, Carrie gave her a tight hug. "We'll never be able to thank you."

"We can try. Have you thought about whether you'd like to go to college?" Brian asked.

"You're kidding!"

"No, I'm not. You think about it, all right?"

Lisa's eyes were shiny as she nodded, then waddled down the corridor to the guest bedroom.

"Do you think we can count on this?" Carrie asked Brian. "I'm almost afraid to."

Tugging her to him, he enfolded her into his arms. It felt so good to feel his strength, to be one in the moment. "It will work out," he assured her.

"I'm afraid to get too excited. What if she changes her mind?"

"I think she made a decision so she knows where she can go from here. If she doesn't want college, maybe there's some other kind of training school she'd like to go to. But the bottom line is we're going to have a baby, Mrs. Summers." He leaned back and gave Carrie a real smile. The Brian smile that had first weakened her knees.

She grinned back until the reality hit her. "We have to get ready! Her due date's in three weeks. There's so much to do—a nursery, a layette—"

"We'll get it all done," Brian soothed. "In fact, we can probably accomplish the nursery in one night. I've got to get back to my office now, but I can be home around six. Look up baby stores in the phone book and pick out the one you want to go to. We'll choose the furniture tonight."

Carrie couldn't believe Brian was going to be home that early. She couldn't believe he was going to spend the evening with her. This baby *was* going to change their lives.

When Brian bent his head to kiss her, Carrie felt tears well up. His lips were gentle on hers at first, then he deepened the kiss. She felt his intensity and hunger and need.

As he reluctantly broke away, she felt shaken. Her response to him had left her trembling. "I'm looking forward to tonight." She felt almost bold as she said it.

He ran his thumb over her bottom lip. "So am I." The desire in his voice made her heart leap.

"See you tonight," he promised and then headed for the door.

That evening Carrie stood next to Brian as he examined a crib. She could smell the spicy scent of his shaving soap. He'd come home about quarter of six, taken a shower and changed, and driven them to first one store and then this one. He was wearing his black leather bomber jacket and black jeans tonight and looked so sexy her tummy did somersaults every time she looked at him. Electrical current from this afternoon was still sparking between them.

As she stood close to him now, acutely aware of his six-two height, his broad shoulders, his strong arms, she asked, "What do you think about this one?"

"I like the walnut finish for a boy. I also like the fact that once he grows out of the crib, we can buy a bed to go with the suite. The changing table will turn into a chest and the dresser will be perfect for a growing boy."

Already Brian was thinking about their child growing up. "He won't be out of the crib for at least two years," she teased.

"Maybe we should buy the bed, too, and store it until he's ready for it."

She could see her husband was completely serious.

He always liked to be prepared and never wanted to be taken by surprise.

Thoughts of the crib and a bed trailed away as she saw a couple walking down the aisle on the other side of the bedroom furniture. Her heart almost stopped as she recognized the woman—Lori Dutera, the counselor her mother had found for her after her abortion.

Since her modeling career had taken off, Carrie had found an apartment in Portland after her high-school graduation. It had amazed her that she could afford one and still send lots of money home to her family. During her senior year in high school, her agent had gotten her shoots in New York, L.A. and London. They'd been handled on weekends and over holidays. That summer after graduation she'd become a model full-time, but in August her life had changed forever.

Carrie hadn't experienced flashbacks in years, but seeing Lori triggered memories she'd wanted to bury.

The August night that summer had been damp, with a drizzle in the humid air. Yet, after a late photo shoot, Carrie had felt the need to walk—to let her hair curl where it wanted to and not worry what she looked like when she got to her own doorstep. Two blocks from her apartment house, it had happened.

Her breath stilled in her chest as the vision of a man wearing a black ski mask returned. She remembered thinking how ludicrous he looked in August. That had been her last coherent thought until she'd stumbled back into her apartment an hour later and locked the door. Not only locked it, but barricaded it with a chair and an end table. She'd felt so unsafe. That was about all she'd felt because everything else had gone numb.

Reliving it all again, she recalled stumbling to her

bedroom and then into the shower, not even stripping off her clothes until the hot water had beat down on her. She'd stripped and soaped herself over and over again. Still tears hadn't come, because she'd shut down. She never even remembered getting out of the shower. She never remembered crawling into bed.

The following morning when the phone rang, she'd been chilled and the sheets had been damp. She'd supposed she'd never dried off. She hadn't intended to pick up the receiver but somehow her mother's voice on her answering machine had cut into the fog surrounding her, and she'd reached for the phone reflexively, as if it were a lifeline. When her mother had asked her what was wrong, she couldn't tell her. She could only cry.

After Paula Bradley attempted to make any sense of what her daughter had said and hadn't said, she'd gotten into the new car Carrie's earnings had bought and driven to Portland from the town of Windsor almost an hour and a half away. Leaving Whitney, who was then sixteen, in charge of her two younger sisters, Mary and Brenda, Paula had told her husband to keep watch on them. He might be disabled and had trouble getting around, but he could lift the phone to call a neighbor if he needed help.

Paula had banged on her daughter's apartment door until Carrie finally looked through the peephole and opened it. Then she'd collapsed in her mother's arms.

Somehow her mother had gotten the story out of Carrie. There was no talk of going to the police. Paula had insisted they shouldn't tell anyone—Carrie's reputation was at stake, her modeling career was at stake. That modeling career was now paying most of the Bradleys' bills. Her mother had insisted on taking her back to

Windsor. There, all she said to the rest of the family was that Carrie was exhausted, sick and needed time to rest.

The only person she'd confided in was Carrie's agent, Ian MacGregor, who'd cleared Carrie's schedule. However, three weeks later when Carrie began losing her breakfast, her mother bought a pregnancy test and confirmed the worst possible news—her daughter was pregnant. With Carrie's future on the line as well as the family's, Paula had known what to do about that, too. She'd had a friend whose daughter had gotten into trouble at fifteen and they'd found a doctor who could do an abortion cheaply.

It had been done cheaply, all right, Carrie thought now, coming back to the present with sheer force of willpower, looking back at that summer instead of reliving it. Three days later, she'd spiked a hundred-and-five-degree fever. The doctor who had performed the abortion prescribed antibiotics. Slowly, she'd physically recovered, but emotionally she'd felt dead. She hadn't eaten or slept, and she couldn't leave the house.

In time, her mother took a different tack and drove Carrie back to her apartment in Portland. There, through a rape crisis center she'd found Lori Dutera and had gone with Carrie to therapy sessions every day for a week. When her mom was sure Carrie could and would keep the appointments on her own, her mother had returned home, yet called Carrie twice a day or more. With the help of Lori, Carrie had turned a nasty corner in her life and finally had seen rays of sunshine again. Each day she'd become stronger until finally, when Ian had called her in January and asked if she would consider modeling for a shampoo ad, she'd said yes.

That commercial had gotten her back into the business

again. That spot had led to a contract with Modern Woman, a nationwide cosmetics company. Safe modeling, her agent had called it, being as protective of her as he would his own daughter. With Modern Woman, she didn't have anything to do with low cleavage or skimpy clothes. She had always dressed elegantly, classically and had been proud of the image. Lori had helped her achieve that.

Carrie hadn't seen the psychologist since her relationship with Foster Garrett had ended. After Foster had walked out of her life, her appointments with Lori had become less frequent. By the time she'd met Brian, she was no longer in therapy.

Now Lori's gaze met hers, and abrupt recognition dawned. The brunette stopped, and the man by her side stopped with her. Lori looked to be around seven months pregnant. Though nearly forty now, she still wore her dark-brown hair in a braid down her back. The glow on her face said her happiness was due to her pregnancy.

When the couple halted on the other side of the crib, Brian switched his focus from the furniture to them.

Lori said simply, "Hi, Carrie. It's been a while."

"About six years," Carrie agreed, suddenly incredibly calm. She knew the counselor would give nothing away. Because Lori had once known everything about her, because they'd become friends of sorts back then, Carrie explained, "This is my husband, Brian. Brian, this is Lori Dutera."

After Lori introduced her husband, Vince, she said easily, "It was good to see you again," and the Duteras moved on.

"An old friend?" Brian asked.

Keep it simple, Carrie reminded herself. Blocking out the events that had led up to meeting Lori, trying to forget the anguish and the pain, she responded, "Yes, an old friend. We've fallen out of touch over the years."

Then acting as if the encounter had meant nothing to her at all, she rested her hand on the crib rail beside Brian's. "I think you're right about buying the bed to go with this now."

He grinned at her. "Great minds think alike. Let's see how soon we can have it all delivered."

An hour later Brian coasted his sedan into the garage, switched off the ignition, and then unsnapped his seat belt. He knew Carrie had been as excited as he had been after Lisa had made her proclamation this afternoon. But after buying the baby furniture, his wife had gone very quiet.

"What are you thinking about?" he asked as she unbuckled her shoulder harness.

Her expression showed surprise that he'd asked. He obviously didn't do that enough.

"I guess the awesome responsibility of what we're about to do is finally hitting me."

The sedan's leather seats had an armrest between them. Raising the armrest, Brian moved closer to her and encircled her shoulders with his arm. "I think we're ready for it, don't you?"

"I hope so. It's just that raising a child is about more than furnishing a nursery. Neither of us came from the ideal situation. I'm hoping we know enough to be good parents."

"I have no doubt you're going to be a fantastic mother. You practiced with your sisters." Carrie's mother had cleaned houses to supplement her husband's disability checks. That had pushed Carrie to grow up quickly and take on more responsibility than a child should have to bear.

"My dad would have been a better father if my mother hadn't left," Brian admitted, thinking about how his upbringing compared to hers.

Carrie shifted toward him. She was wearing a hooded fleece jacket tonight. She was soft and feminine and always smelled of a flower garden. Leaning against his shoulder, she suggested, "Your dad could never get past the bitterness of your mom leaving. I think he gambled to forget. Maybe if he'd looked for love again—"

"He wasn't taking any chances on a woman again and I don't blame him. My mother betrayed him. He could never trust anybody again." The past was something Brian didn't like to talk about, and he wasn't sure how they'd tumbled into the conversation now.

He brushed his jaw against the top of Carrie's head. "We're going to make good parents." Shifting toward her, he studied her. She was so very beautiful, so very sincere, so very…good. He'd needed that, and right now he needed her.

"We should go in," he said with a decided lack of conviction.

"I know," she murmured, not moving away.

His lips rested against her temple, tasting her skin. He breathed in her scent. It was intoxicatingly seductive as he kissed her cheekbone.

"Brian," she whispered.

He heard something in the sound of his name that stopped him. Leaning back, he studied her once more. "Is something wrong?"

"No! No. I'm just so grateful for you, for your gentleness. It takes my breath away sometimes. That's all."

Her words triggered a fire that fueled his passion for her. Sliding his hand into her hair, he tipped her head back and sealed his lips to hers.

It took a moment until Brian could feel Carrie respond to the kiss, respond to him. Kissing Carrie always shook him because emotion rose up that he usually kept at bay. Hunger tried to escape the confines of his tight control. Need became a flaw he didn't want to recognize. When he kissed Carrie, he felt powerful and weak at the same time. The irony of that unsettled him. Tonight, however, with the knowledge that they'd soon be parenting a child together, with the family he'd always wanted becoming a reality, he let nature take its course.

The innate attraction they'd always felt for each other pushed away everything else. When he unzipped Carrie's jacket, she didn't protest and when her hand slipped below his belt, he didn't stop her. As he caressed her breast, she pressed her palm against his erection. Groaning, he slid his tongue over her teeth, exploring every erotic zone in her mouth.

The light that had automatically gone on when the garage door was activated suddenly went out, and they were plunged into darkness. He felt Carrie's intake of breath. She liked light. Even when she went to bed she always kept on the nightlight in the bathroom off the bedroom. Her hand had stilled the moment the garage had gone dark.

Enfolding her closer to him, he broke the kiss. "We really should go in. Lisa probably heard the garage door go up. She could come out and check any minute to see what we're doing."

"She's probably watching TV," Carrie murmured.

Brian switched on the map light under the dashboard

and gazed at his wife, smoothing her hair behind her ear. "Lisa could take one look at you and know what we've been doing." His wife's lips were pink and swollen, her hair was mussed from his fingers running through it. She was flushed, too.

"I don't think she'd be shocked," Carrie said lightly.

"I agree it would probably take a lot to shock her, but I don't want to talk about Lisa. I'd rather go up to our bedroom and finish what we started."

His body was demanding release. From the bright sparkle in Carrie's eyes and the heat in her cheeks, he suspected she'd still be in the mood, too, when they got upstairs.

"I'll leave the dashlight on until you get inside."

He'd intended to kiss her one last time before she left the car, except his cell phone rang. Pulling it off the charger attached under the dash, he answered automatically, "Summers Development."

When Carrie heard him say, "Hi, Rob. No, I didn't pick up my messages. I've been busy." She pointed to the door leading into the kitchen, signaling to Brian that she was going to go inside.

He nodded.

Climbing out of the car, Carrie closed the door as quietly as she could, went up the step, turned off the alarm system, walked past the mudroom and entered the kitchen.

After she'd seen Lori in the furniture store, she'd tried everything in her power to keep old memories from coming alive again. She was done with all of that now. She'd gone on, although she'd always be thankful for the help Lori had given her. Her therapist's insights and wise guidance had helped Carrie rebuild her life.

Still, it was hard to shake off the shadows that had engulfed her when she'd seen Lori again, and Brian must have sensed something.

For a few seconds in the car, she'd thought about telling him, recounting all of it. But then they'd slid into the conversation about their parents. She had no doubt that Brian would feel betrayed she'd never confided in him about all of it, especially because of the infertility problems. He'd never forgive her, just as he hadn't forgiven his mother. They were becoming closer again...

While Carrie waited for Brian, she looked in on Lisa. The teenager was watching TV and just waved at her. Carrie sensed she didn't want to be disturbed. After an "I'll see you in the morning," Carrie returned to the kitchen to make a snack for her and Brian to take upstairs. She needed Brian tonight. She needed his strength and his gentleness as well as his conviction that they'd be good parents.

When Brian came in from the garage, his expression was serious. He saw the dish of cheese, crackers and fruit Carrie had prepared and he grimaced. "I won't be coming to bed for a while. I'm expecting a fax any minute, then I have to put some figures together."

Her disappointment must have shown.

"The owner of the Hawaiian property has decided to sell," he explained. "I won't have to fly there now, but I will in a few weeks."

Her mind still swirling between the past and the future, Carrie asked, "Can't you send someone else? Lisa's baby will probably be born by then."

"Let's handle this one day at a time. If I do have to go, maybe you and the baby can go with me. It would be our first vacation as a family."

"Except it wouldn't be a vacation for you. You'd be working," she protested.

"Not all the time. Maybe a few days out of the week. Just think about it."

"Will *you* think about delegating the responsibility to someone else so you don't have to go?" She'd never expressed her opinion about this before. When it was just the two of them, it seemed to be her job to support whatever Brian did. But now, with a baby…

Brian's response could determine the course of their future as well as the course of their marriage.

Five

"It's not that simple, Carrie," Brian replied, not giving her the answer she wanted.

"Maybe it would be that simple if you were willing to let go of a little control." Something had happened to her when she'd seen Lori tonight. She'd remembered she needed to fight for what she wanted.

"I didn't get where I am by letting go of control."

"And where are you, Brian? Where are *we*? You have enough investments to retire comfortably now. Once we have a baby, don't you want to be a *real* father?"

"Real? What is a *real* father?" he asked warily.

"A *real* father is available twenty-four hours a day, seven days a week. A real father knows his son or daughter's birthday, goes to soccer games, helps with homework. A real father knows his child inside out and if there's something wrong, there's no way he'd miss it."

Her father had never known about her rape, had just accepted the explanation that Carrie had taken a break from modeling because she'd gotten the flu and needed time off.

"What did your father miss?" Brian asked perceptively.

Her husband's question was an opening if she wanted to take it, but the mood between them had definitely been broken. Brian might have always wanted an ideal family, but her concept of ideal parents and his might be very different. She couldn't confide in him when she felt as if they were miles apart. She couldn't confide in him knowing he didn't forgive mistakes easily. What she had done was much more than a mistake, and she'd never forgive herself for it. How could she expect anybody else to?

"My father wasn't so different from yours. After he was hurt, he was lost in his pain and painkillers. Your father blamed your mother for his lot in life. My father blamed fate."

The fax machine in Brian's office beeped. Carrie could hear the sound of the document printing out.

When Brian approached Carrie, she held out the plate of cheese, fruit and crackers. "Take this with you. You might get hungry while you're working."

"Don't you want any?"

"I'm not hungry. I'll settle in with a book I started."

"There's always tomorrow night," Brian suggested easily.

"Unless you get another unexpected phone call."

Several emotions played across her husband's face, and she couldn't sort them out. She knew the way Dutch Summers had left one job for another and gambled money away. Brian was determined never to let that happen to him and had developed a work ethic that superseded all else. But if they had a child, his life wouldn't be so black and white.

To her surprise, Brian nudged up her chin and kissed her long and hard. Then he stepped away.

Moments later, he'd gone into his office and she knew he'd be working half the night.

Brian was studying a list of architects who might want to bid on designing the resort in Hawaii when the security alarm went off. His first thought was that Carrie had been right with her preoccupation to make sure the system was always set.

Pushing his chair back quickly, he was ready to take on whoever had breached their home. Then common sense prevailed. Possibly an animal on the patio had set off the motion detector. That had happened before.

When he hurried to the family room, he realized immediately a stray cat had had nothing to do with setting off the alarm. Lisa had. She stood at the open French doors, looking panicked.

"Stay put," he told her as he went to the kitchen door that led to the garage, opened the panel just inside the door and punched in a code that turned off the alarm. When the phone rang, he picked up the cordless phone in the kitchen, taking it with him to the family room.

"It was a false alarm," he told the security personnel, reciting his ID number so they'd know he wasn't a burglar giving them a reason not to answer the alarm.

After he finished with the security company, Brian went to the stairs and called up to his wife. "Carrie, there's nothing to worry about. Lisa set it off."

"I'll be right down," she called back.

When he returned to the family room, he found Lisa still standing just inside the French doors. She was wearing a red hooded jacket that Carrie had bought her to replace her tattered, dirty one.

"Where were you going?" Brian demanded, checking his watch and seeing it was one in the morning.

"I just needed some fresh air," she returned defiantly.

He saw she had her purse under her arm and she was in full makeup. "You're in no condition to be out in the city at night. If you're going to live here, I expect the truth from you, even if it gets you in trouble."

"So what if I get in trouble with you? Are you going to put me back out on the streets? I'm eighteen, Mr. Summers. I can do whatever the hell I want."

"Where were you going, Lisa?" He wouldn't let her sidetrack him from the issue. If she was going to run away again because everything had gotten to be too much to handle, he and Carrie would just have to deal with that.

"I was going to meet a friend."

Carrie suddenly appeared beside him, and he wondered how much of the exchange she'd heard.

"If you're not going to think about yourself," she said softly, "you've got to think about your baby. What if you had a dizzy spell on your way somewhere? How were you going to get where you want to go?"

Lisa raised her chin. "I was going to walk out of the development and catch a bus."

"Lisa…" Carrie's voice was so gentle, Brian saw that it got to the girl. *Carrie* got to the girl.

"Were you going to meet someone?" she asked, fully expecting an answer.

"My best friend, Ariel," Lisa confessed with a catch in her voice. "She hasn't been able to find a job and she doesn't have any family, either."

"Where were you going to meet her?"

"At the shelter. I was going to throw stones at the window and then she'd let me in."

Standing beside Lisa now, Carrie suggested, "If you want to meet your friend, call the shelter and set up a time. I'll take you to see her."

"You'd do that?"

"Sure. I'm volunteering at the hospital in the morning, but I'm free in the afternoon. You can even meet her at the mall for lunch, my treat."

Lisa eyed Brian. "I wasn't going to run away. I would have come back."

He didn't know whether to believe her or not. "I set the security alarm when I come home at night. If you have plans after that, you'll have to let us know."

"That sounds a little bit like being kept in jail," Lisa returned solemnly.

"Your idea of jail is somebody else's idea of security."

"I feel safer knowing we have a security system and it's on at night," Carrie explained.

After Lisa looked down at her sneakers, she seemed less defiant. "I guess I'll go to bed. I'll try to get hold of Ariel early tomorrow morning. At breakfast I'll let you know what time we're going to meet."

Carrie nodded.

As Lisa headed for her room, Brian made sure the French doors were locked. "I don't trust her." Deep worry twisted in his gut. "She could take off at any time and there's nothing we can do about it."

"I don't think she wants to run away. As she said, I

think she's feeling trapped. We have to believe her, Brian, or else trust will never grow."

He ran his fingers through his hair. "She might want to stay involved in her baby's life. We have to consider that, too." Now that the first glow of the idea of adopting had worn off, they had to face the reality of what they were doing.

"I've read a lot of material on open adoptions since we've been considering this," Carrie said, "and they're usually best for everybody concerned. I truly don't think Lisa wants to be a mother and I don't think she'll want to be one anytime in the near future."

"So you'd be okay with her dropping in and out of this baby's life?"

Carrie's dark eyes were luminous with emotion. "Yes, because *we'll* be the parents. *We'll* be caring for him day and night. If Lisa wants to visit, that's fine, because *we'll* be the mom and dad."

Brian knew many women would feel competitive with Lisa and threatened by her, but Carrie was thinking of this child's welfare and he admired her for that. "Are you going back to bed?"

"Yes. I think I'd just fallen asleep."

He remembered the way their evening had ended abruptly. "I'll be up in about an hour."

Carried nodded but didn't say she'd wait up.

When Carrie left the family room, Brian thought about going with her and easing the need in his body that hadn't diminished. But he had a responsibility to anyone who wanted to invest in the Hawaiian project, and he needed to put together a package on it by the weekend. Thinking about what Carrie had said, he considered delegating and letting go of some of the control.

Could he do that? Maybe Ted would want a more ac-
tive role. Brian couldn't imagine bringing somebody
new in to be his right-hand man. It took too long to build
up a working relationship, too long to establish the trust
he'd need to delegate. Could Ted handle the responsibility of heading up new projects?

Brian knew if he tried to figure that out now, he'd be
up all night.

When Carrie returned home from the hospital the
next day, she was glad she had taken time to read to the
children. They'd helped her put other distractions out of
her head. Last night when the security alarm had gone
off, she'd awakened in a panic, then broken into a cold
sweat. For a moment, the fear that someone had broken
in and was going to hurt her, violate her again, had frozen her and filled her with terror. Then Brian had called
up the steps.

She'd taken about ten deep breaths, brushed her
hair and come downstairs as if nothing had happened.
So many times she'd weighed Brian's right to know
about her past with the consequences of telling him.
Foster had turned away. Wouldn't Brian turn away, too?
Wouldn't any man? Not only because she'd had an abortion, but because the infection from that abortion had
spoiled all of her plans to have a family?

After she had taken the antibiotic the doctor had
given her and recovered, she'd never known about the
scarring from the infection. It hadn't been until she'd
gone to the fertility specialist, had tests and confided in
him about the abortion that she'd learned the extent of
the damage.

Brian had taken to the idea of adoption slowly, but

now he was embracing it as much as she was. She was so grateful for that and for Lisa, she was willing to do whatever she could to help the teenager find her life.

When Carrie checked on Lisa, she found her getting dressed. Carrie told her to take her time and she went to the kitchen. The housekeeper had been in that morning and homey smells of cooked food swirled around the kitchen. As Carrie peeked into the refrigerator, she found glazed chicken pieces in a casserole with a note to warm it at 350 degrees for forty-five minutes. There were steamed fresh vegetables to reheat in the microwave, and bread pudding cooled on the counter. Carrie had gotten the recipe from Verna for that and had tried it on her own a few times. She liked cooking and had done it a lot for her family when she'd lived at home. But cooking for one seemed to be a waste of time with Brian rarely home for dinner. Maybe that would change now. Maybe Lisa would join them at dinner and they could have a "family" meal. Carrie realized she wanted that almost as much as she wanted Brian to be home more often. Usually she didn't voice her opinion about that or his long hours, but last night with a baby to consider, she'd felt she'd had to say something.

Checking the answering machine, she found a message from Leigh Bartlett. Leigh and her husband, Adam, were inviting Carrie and Brian to come riding at their ranch on Saturday and to stay for dinner. That would be fun. *If* Brian didn't have other plans.

Carrie was pouring herself a glass of apple juice when the phone rang. Picking it up with an unhurried "Hello," she heard, "Carrie, it's Mom. I'm glad I caught you."

Since she was eighteen, Carrie had had mixed feelings about her mother. Counseling had helped in that regard. At first, Carrie had blamed herself for the rape and the abortion. She shouldn't have been walking home alone at night. She should have been wearing something less provocative. She should have realized what could happen to a young woman on the streets and somehow prevented it. She should have been stronger after the rape, pulled herself together, gone to the police, reclaimed her life. She should never have let her mother talk her into an abortion.

Lori had helped her look at each of those statements from different angles. Her therapist had explained post-traumatic stress syndrome and assured Carrie that women handled rape differently—some wanted to hide and never see the light of day again. During the first three months of counseling, Lori had helped Carrie understand that her mother's fears had played into the situation, too. Paula Bradley had seen her oldest daughter as her family's salvation. Ever since her husband had been disabled, they'd lived on government checks that hadn't gone far with four girls to raise. Cleaning money had also gone for basic expenses.

When Carrie's modeling career had taken off, all that had changed. Her mother could finally meet the bills and even buy new clothes. They'd made plans to move into a bigger apartment in a better part of town and they'd bought a new car. Carrie's father owned a bigger TV and had subscriptions to sports magazines he'd never been able to afford. He also had a refrigerator stocked with beer and had seemed to shake himself out of the depression he'd experienced since his accident. He'd even seemed happy at times. Even more than the rape, her mother had seen Carrie's pregnancy as a severe threat to the lifestyle they were starting to enjoy.

She didn't want any of her daughters to end up cleaning other people's houses. She didn't want to go back to counting pennies, stretching macaroni casseroles, or worrying if they could pay next month's rent. She'd seen an abortion as Carrie's only way out, as her family's only way out.

Over and over Lori had insisted that no one should make a decision under stress, especially not one that would affect the rest of her life. Furthermore, she'd decided that Carrie hadn't even made a *conscious* decision. She'd been in a state of shock, still reliving the rape and the horror of being violated. In a way, her mother had taken advantage of Carrie's emotional state. Back then, Carrie had had trouble accepting Lori's reasoning. She still did to a certain extent. She felt *she* was responsible for her own decisions. Yet, if her mother hadn't come to her "rescue," she knew she would never have had the abortion. Even now, it was all still confusing. Even now, she still blamed herself. Although she'd decided long ago to forgive her mother for whatever part she'd played in everything that had happened, the experience had raised a wall between them.

Carrie usually spoke to her mother every few weeks. She and Brian had gone to Windsor for Christmas. "Hi, Mom, how are you?"

"I'm fine. How are you?"

"I'm good." Although she'd told Brenda about Lisa and the possibility of becoming a mother soon, she hesitated to go into it with her mom.

After a few moments of silence, her mother filled the void. "I just wanted to thank you again for the generous Christmas presents you and Brian gave us. Your dad loves his recliner, and I took the leather handbag you gave me to a meeting at church. Everybody oohed and aahed over it. The coat, too. It's such a pretty color of ruby."

Once Carrie had signed the contract with Modern Woman Cosmetics, she'd invested in a house in Windsor where her mom and dad could live for the rest of their lives rent-free. As she'd made more money, she'd set up a trust for her parents. Her mother no longer had to clean other people's homes, though she insisted on working as a cashier at a local drugstore.

"I'm glad you like the gifts. I put the scarves you embroidered in the bedroom. Brian took the travel alarm to San Francisco last week."

"Did you go along?"

"No, something came up."

"It must have been something important to keep you from going with him."

"I guess it was." Taking a deep breath, she launched into the subject she'd avoided discussing with her mom. "Brian and I finished all the prerequisites for adopting a child. We found out that an unwed mother needed a place to stay during the last month of her pregnancy, and we offered to let her stay here. It looks as if we're going to adopt her baby."

This time the silence between mother and daughter was palpable. Finally her mother asked, "You've given up trying to have a child of your own?"

"I have no choice, Mom."

"You blame me because you can't have children, don't you?"

Carrie's response was automatic. "No, I don't."

"I think you do."

"Mom, let's not get into this again. Brian and I are going to have a baby. He'll be your grandson. Can you be happy about that?"

"I did what was best, Carrie," Paula Bradley said for the millionth time. "I did it for your sake as much as for the money you could bring into the family with your modeling career. What would have happened to you? Where would your future have gone? You were already somebody important, getting your picture in all those magazines, flying off to New York and Europe. I didn't want that to end for you."

Maybe it was time for her to express her feelings to her mother, too. "Mom, look. I understand what you did and why you did it. You thought the abortion would be best for everyone. But now I understand the abortion wasn't best for me, even without the infertility problems. It was *my* fault more than yours. I should have stood up to you. I should have figured out a way to keep my baby *and* my career."

"I think you were too young to do that," her mother murmured. "I never should have let you live in Portland by yourself."

There was so much blame, plenty to go around. It was time it stopped, at least where she and her mother were concerned. She knew her own guilt would never leave her, but she'd deal with that. "As much as we want to, we can't go back and change anything. Through all the counseling, at least I learned that. Now that Brian and I are going to have a baby, I want you to look forward to being a grandma again."

Paula sighed. "I didn't think it would ever happen for you. When's the baby due?"

"February second. But you know how that goes. I

guess he can come late or early. I'll let you know as soon as he's born."

"Will you?"

"Yes. Brian and I will take tons of pictures so you don't miss a thing. As soon as we can, we'll visit."

"I'd like that. So would your dad."

"Good. Brian's pretty busy right now, but maybe I can get up to see you and Whitney, Mary and the kids within the next couple of weeks."

"Just let me know when you're coming and I'll bake that lemon pudding cake you like so much."

"I'll do that."

A few moments later, Carrie had said goodbye and reached for her apple juice. She'd been standing in the corner facing the cabinets while she and her mother talked. Now as she turned, she saw Lisa in the doorway to the kitchen. How long had she been there?

"You went to counseling?" Lisa asked.

A cold shiver skittered up Carrie's spine. She'd mentioned the counseling at the end of her discussion with her mom. "Yes, I did. It helped during a very confusing time in my life."

"Something like I'm going through now?"

Relieved, Carrie realized Lisa hadn't heard the earlier part of the conversation. "When you don't know which direction to turn, it's good to ask for help. A counselor is one way to go. The caseworker you consulted with is another."

"I'm not thinking about the pregnancy so much, but I still really miss my folks. I still wake up in the middle of the night sometimes crying. It's been three years. That's not normal, is it?"

"I doubt if you'll ever stop missing them. The missing might become less painful and you'll remember the good times. At least that's what I understand about grief, about losing somebody. Whenever you lose someone, they take a piece of your heart with them so you can't expect to ever be the same as you were before. My counselor explained that to me one time."

"I guess you can try to replace that piece."

"I guess you can, but even if you replace it, the new piece doesn't fit exactly and there's still that space for the missing. But it keeps you connected, too. If you didn't miss your parents, maybe then you wouldn't feel how much you love them and how much they loved you."

Lisa had placed her purse on the table and now she picked it up. "I'm ready to go whenever you are."

"I'm ready. I was thinking maybe after your lunch with Ariel, we might want to shop for some new clothes for you. What do you think?"

"You're buying?" Lisa asked with a mischievous grin.

"I'm buying," Carrie assured her.

"Can we stop at the makeup counter, too?"

With a smile, feeling like a big sister, Carrie wrapped her arm around the girl's shoulders. "Sure we can."

She was really looking forward to their excursion to the mall.

The sun played hide-and-seek with the January clouds as Brian nudged his horse into a run on Saturday afternoon. His burst of speed surprised Carrie. He was hatless, wearing a flannel shirt and an insulated vest to give him freedom of movement. His jean-clad legs were close to the horse's sides as he leaned lower in the saddle and became one with the horse. This break in their normal routine, horseback riding at Adam and

Leigh Bartlett's ranch, was a break they didn't take often enough. Maybe relaxing this afternoon and evening could dissolve the discord between them.

Carrie had known Leigh for over two years. They'd become friends when one of the children in the pediatric ward had been transferred to the oncology unit. Leigh was a pediatric oncology nurse. When Leigh had married Adam Bartlett, the two of them had decided to turn his ranch into a camp for kids with cancer. They were in the process of doing that now and the first children were slated to arrive in the summer.

The overwhelming urge to catch up with Brian overtook Carrie and thoughts of Leigh and Adam slipped aside as she flicked her horse's reins, leaned low over the bay gelding, and encouraged, "Let's catch up to him." Carrie had learned to ride when she'd done a magazine shoot and stayed on a ranch in Jackson Hole, Wyoming. She'd loved being around the horses, grooming them, taking lessons from the rancher's wife. In two weeks she'd gone from greenhorn to novice rider. When she'd returned to Portland, she'd ridden at a nearby stable as often as she could. After she'd married Brian, she'd been pleased to learn he'd spent some time around horses whenever he visited a friend in Salinas who had a ranch there. They'd ridden together on occasion during the first year of their marriage, but then…it had stopped.

Now all Carrie could think about was not letting Brian get too far ahead of her. He was streaking forward on a chestnut gelding named Raider as if he were glued to him, as if rushing through the wind at breakneck speed was something Brian had longed to do for a lifetime. She knew the feeling. She knew the freedom of being one with the horse, trusting him as he trusted her, practically flying through time and space.

Gripping her horse's mane, she urged him, "Faster, Samson. We have to show him we can keep up." That was all-important to her now, proving to Brian she was his partner and his equal.

When she pulled even with Brian, he glanced at her as if surprised. A few moments later he pulled out ahead of her again and kept his lead. There was a copse of pines up ahead and Brian slowed as he neared it. She did, too, and finally came to a stop next to him.

"That was wonderful," she breathed, feeling exhilarated.

"Yes, it was. I didn't think you'd race me, though. I was going to give Raider a good workout, then turn around and come back to you."

"You didn't think I'd enjoy a good race?" she asked jokingly. There was a bit of seriousness behind it, too.

"I didn't know if you'd be secure enough in the saddle to flat-out run. We haven't done much of it lately."

"No, we haven't, and I think we ought to take up Leigh and Adam on the offer to come out and ride more often."

"Didn't I hear Leigh say she'd be glad to baby-sit while we rode?"

"Yes, but if we have a baby, I just can't imagine leaving him in somebody else's hands."

"Maybe we can come out again next weekend if the weather holds."

"That's one advantage of adopting," she said lightly. "If I were pregnant, you'd have to ride alone."

"If you were pregnant, I'd be home watching over you."

She didn't know what had even made her bring it up.

She shouldn't have because she saw a fleeting shadow cross Brian's face and knew he longed for a wife who could get pregnant with his own child. Was she deluding herself into thinking anything would change after they had Lisa's baby in their arms? Could Brian really accept the baby as his? What if this adoption fell through? What would happen to them then?

Breaking eye contact, she patted her horse's neck and she could feel Brian's gaze on her. Swallowing hard, she said, "I'd better walk him."

Brian looked up at the sky. "That sun could disappear altogether and we could end up with rain again."

With the subject changed, remnants of things unsaid still wafted between them.

Turning his horse toward the ranch, Brian started back, waiting for her to follow. But instead of following as she once might have done, she pulled up beside him.

Six

When Carrie and Brian returned to the corral, Adam was waiting for them with a grin. "I'll help you groom Samson and Raider while Leigh puts the finishing touches on dinner. She wants me to show you the house for the kids."

Carrie liked Adam as much as she did Leigh. He was a self-made man like Brian. From what Leigh had told her, he had come from a harsh childhood to become CEO of his own software company. He still kept his hand in Novel Programs Unlimited's workings but for the most part now, he let his partner handle the day-to-day running of the company while he and Leigh put all of their energy and attention into getting this camp for kids with cancer up and running.

"You've built another barn, too," Carrie noted, her enthusiasm for his project showing.

"With three barns and two houses, you're going to need a good bit of staff," Brian added.

"Leigh's in the process of interviewing now. I'm trying to find a good horse trainer to help me choose the right mounts for the kids."

"Does Thunder still have his own barn and corral?" Thunder was Adam's spirited stallion.

"No. There are two other geldings with him now and they calmed him down. Leigh even rides him on occasion. She and that horse seemed to have developed a special bond. But I still won't let a stranger on him."

As Brian and Carrie dismounted, Adam led them into the barn. The smell of hay, old wood and leather cleaner was pleasurable to Carrie. Soon she and Adam were brushing down Samson while Brian worked on Raider.

"I feel comfortable and safe in a barn," Carrie mused as her hands smoothed over Samson's coat. "Maybe it's because it's so earthy...so real."

"Or maybe you were a cowgirl in a past life," Adam joked.

She laughed. "Maybe. Sometimes I think horses are easier to communicate with than people."

"You won't get an argument on that from me. Until Leigh came back into my life, Thunder was my best friend."

Carrie thought about Leigh and Adam, as well as their life on Cedar Run Ranch. "You're so lucky."

Adam peered at her over Samson's withers. "How so?"

"You can get up in the morning and take a ride if you want. Or when you finish your day, you can just hop on Thunder and clear the cobwebs out of your head."

"Yeah, but don't forget the vet bills and the upkeep,

not to mention the time. Rodney takes care of the horses for me, but I like to handle them myself, exercise them and just generally make sure they're in good shape. Leigh calls it my overseer complex."

Carrie didn't know if Brian, who had been silent up until then, had been paying attention to the conversation. Suddenly he was involved, too. "I don't think it's unusual to want to make sure something you put your time and your heart into flourishes. That's the whole point of working and living, isn't it?" her husband asked seriously.

"I suppose. But I'm going to have to trust someone else to do the overseeing once the kids arrive. Leigh and I want to make sure we give all of our attention to them."

That was the sensitive topic simmering between her and Brian. When she glanced over at him, though, his focus was concentrated on grooming Raider.

Fifteen minutes later, Adam's excitement was contagious as he showed them around the new barn and then the house, which could sleep about twelve children. The rooms were cheery, with lots of primary colors in the wallpaper and borders.

As Adam took them on the grand tour of the upstairs, he explained, "We'll have one full-time housemother and she'll have two aides. It depends how many children we house at one time. With Leigh being our program director and resident nurse, she'll be busy with planning and monitoring the kids. I intend to just be around, roughhouse with them, play football and generally get in the way."

"How's your brother Mark?" Brian asked.

"He's doing well and on his way to a full recovery. It's been a long haul, but every time I see him now, he looks healthier."

Adam had never known his real father, Jared Cambry. Last year, his dad had found him because Adam was the only hope for a bone marrow transplant for Jared's youngest son Mark. Fortunately, Adam had been a perfect match. Through it all, he'd gained a family he'd never really had.

"Will Mark be coming to the camp?"

"I hope so. Maybe by the end of the summer."

Brian had wandered to the windows overlooking the back of the house. "Are you going to cut a trail through those woods for hiking?"

"We plan to. Actually, I'm going to clear a few more of those trees so we can put equipment in the backyard—a jungle gym, swings, a slide."

"Are you going to do it yourself?"

"Yes. Toward the end of the week." After a short pause, he added, jokingly, "I can always use an extra hand. Especially splitting the logs afterward."

"I'd be glad to help," Brian offered. "I haven't swung an axe for a few years but I heard it's like riding a bike, something you never forget."

"Are you serious?" Adam asked.

"Sure. That'll be a better physical workout than using the Nautilus."

"You're on," Adam said. "With you helping, we may be able to finish it in a day."

Carrie wasn't surprised Brian had offered to help. He was a physical man and tried to keep fit any way he could. She could see the idea of outside work appealed to him.

After they left the newly built house, they walked down the lane to Adam and Leigh's home. Carrie loved the look of the log home, which was rustic and charming. The walk to the door was lined with split rail fence. When Adam led them inside, Carrie was reminded what a cozy home felt like. There were colorful hand-woven rugs on the hardwood floor, lots of light from a skylight and windows, a casual atmosphere emanating from the rustic beams. All the rooms were on one floor and Carrie knew in addition to the dining room and kitchen, there were three bedrooms and a study. It felt so much homier than her house, so much more lived-in.

As Leigh came in from the kitchen to the living room, Carrie said, "I do love your house."

Leigh had tied back her blond hair into a ponytail. She was wearing jeans, boots and a patterned sweater and looked happier than Carrie had ever seen her. "We love it, too. After you wash up, dinner will be ready."

As Adam and Brian talked during dinner, Carrie realized how much the two men had in common. Brian had always gotten along with Adam, but now it seemed as if a real friendship was growing. He didn't have that with the men he worked with, she knew. He always kept them at arm's length, separating his business life from his personal life.

"Lisa didn't want to come along with you?" Leigh asked Carrie.

When she'd accepted Leigh's invitation, Carrie had told her about Lisa. "She decided she'd rather stay home."

"How long until her due date?"

"Almost three weeks. We ordered furniture for the nursery and it's being delivered in a few days."

"You're going to be busy all the way around. Do you have to do much preparation for hosting the public awareness program for the bone marrow donor registry?"

Carrie was looking forward to the telethon she was emceeing on Tuesday. "I have to go over the backgrounds of the guests I'm going to interview. I'll figure out how to help them open up so they're comfortable. The entertainment is already lined up. We have a pop singer, as well as a band from one of the veterans' organizations. The coordinator of the program seems to know exactly what she's doing. I liked working with her."

"It's been a while since you were in the limelight, hasn't it?" Leigh asked.

"Yes, and I'm a bit nervous about it."

"You've no reason on earth to be nervous," Brian insisted as he reached over and took her hand.

All of a sudden she realized the men's conversation had stopped and somewhere along the way, they had listened in on her conversation with Leigh. "I have to talk for practically ninety minutes straight with only breaks for commercials and entertainment. If I can't get the parents and kids to really open up to me, the audience is going to be bored and no one will call in to register." Brian's hand on hers felt so good. Not only good, but protective and reassuring, too.

"I think I have more confidence in you than you have in yourself," he teased. "You tell stories to the kids at the hospital all the time. You've always been a success emceeing the auction for the Ladies Guild. That's why Linda Jamison chose you for this."

"How do you know that?"

"I have my sources." His smile was crooked, and he looked almost boyish.

"I heard the same thing floating around the hospital," Leigh added. "You have a reputation, Carrie. You're poised and kind and you never seem to offend anyone. I heard you were the first and only choice to hostess this program."

"No pressure here," she said, trying to keep her voice light. Since she'd stopped modeling, she'd never thought about how other people saw her. Except Brian.

To Carrie's relief, Leigh asked if anyone would like seconds. Dessert wasn't far behind. When Adam went into the kitchen to help Leigh fetch it, Brian leaned closer to her. "You aren't really nervous about the program, are you?"

Looking up into his dark-brown eyes, she almost forgot what they were talking about. His blue-and-red flannel shirt was open at the throat, and chest hair whirled there. He'd taken off the vest and she realized how much she liked the way he looked in jeans.

"Carrie?" he asked, an amused smile playing on his lips.

With great effort, she remembered his question. He still smelled like the outdoors and winter and man, and she was caught up in that, too. "I get jittery whenever I think about the program."

"Then you shouldn't think about it until two minutes before you go on."

"Sage advice," she agreed. "Very easy to give, very hard to take."

Still smiling, he murmured, "I guess every time you think about it, we should do something to distract you."

"Like?" she asked, loving this more playful side of her husband, wishing it popped out more often.

"Like this." Slipping his hand under her hair, he bent to her, brushed his lips tantalizingly over hers, and gave them both the pleasure of a full kiss.

Carrie lost track of time and place…lost track of everything but Brian. Hungry desire was always there. Fiery passion took over as soon as his lips met hers. His work had gotten in the way this week, as well as concerns about Lisa, but she also wondered if the last time they'd made love, too much had opened up for both of them—too much need, too much longing, too much desire for something more than what they had.

Breaking the kiss, Brian eased his hand from under her hair and murmured in her ear, "Tonight."

She wondered what tonight would bring. She wondered if the intimacy she so desperately wanted was possible without sharing her deepest secrets with Brian.

She didn't think it was.

She hoped she was wrong.

When Brian stepped into the elevator on Sunday afternoon, he automatically pressed the button for five, his floor of office suites. He hadn't planned to work today. Derrick had called him about going over documents on the Alaskan land deal. He'd seen the disappointed look in Carrie's eyes after he'd taken the call. He didn't understand why she was disappointed. After all, she planned to spend the afternoon with Lisa going over birthing techniques. She couldn't expect him to get involved with that!

Yet maybe she had. His wife was becoming a woman he didn't know. He used to be able to predict her every reaction. But no more. Like yesterday when he realized she intended to race him. She'd never done anything so wild and reckless before. He didn't like her doing it now. Yet that wild side of her intrigued him.

He still didn't understand how she could relate to Lisa so well. They were such opposites. But there was

some kind of bond tying them together. Curious about
the shelter where Lisa had stayed, he'd stopped there before coming to his office. His eyes had been opened to
the problems runaways faced. As he'd spoken to the director, he'd realized there were too many teenagers like
Lisa, not in a shelter but on the streets.

The elevator doors opened and Brian strode to the
double oak doors that led to his office suites. Inserting
one key and then another, he unlocked the doors and
tapped in the security code to turn off the alarm.

The plush slate-gray carpeting, the wine-colored
leather furniture, the contemporary watercolors on the
walls spoke of a decorator's penchant for detail. Usually taking pride in what he had accomplished, today
Brian hardly noticed it as he rounded the receptionist's
U-shaped desk and headed down a corridor. His office
was at the end.

Once more using a key, he let himself inside. Here
gray, navy and teak combined in a space that fit his
every need. Again he took little notice as he opened a
file drawer and found the folder he was looking for.

Though he took it to his desk and sat in the high-back
swivel chair, he didn't open it. Instead, he reached for
his checkbook in the top left drawer. Decision made, he
wrote out a contribution to the shelter that existed
mainly on the kindness of private citizens and corpora-
tions. The director had explained how they tried to help
women get back on their feet rather than just giving
them a roof over their heads and hot food. It was a good
cause, he told himself as he wrote out the check.

It still rankled that Carrie had made the decision to
invite Lisa into their home without even consulting him.
That wasn't like his wife. But then it wasn't like Carrie

to abdicate her role as hostess at one of his business dinners, either. It wasn't like her to introduce him to an old friend then tell him nothing about her. It wasn't like her to back out of a trip to San Francisco, race him on a horse, or tell him that she was afraid their marriage was in trouble if this adoption didn't go through.

Placing the check in the middle of the folder taken from the file cabinet, he swiveled away from it and reached for the portfolio that he'd slid between the bookshelves and the wall. He hadn't gone through it in a very long time. Now drawn to it, he carried it to the conference table, unzipped it and revealed a project that had once been a dream. Somehow he'd turned it into reality. This portfolio held his preliminary sketches and concept ideas drawn before he handed them over to an architect who designed the finished product. There were malls, high-rise office complexes and resorts. In the back of the portfolio, he found sketches he hadn't examined in years.

Usually he didn't draw people. He wasn't an artist. He just had an eye for what kind of buildings fit best on properties. Still…when he'd first met Carrie, she'd gotten under his skin so completely, he'd sketched her several times from memory. Always his worst critic, Brian had to admit the charcoal drawings weren't bad. He'd never shown them to his wife. He'd never considered them worthy of framing. After all, he could pay to have a *real* artist paint her portrait anytime. Yet he found himself studying them, studying Carrie. She'd looked different then—happier. Had he been happier, too? Had striving for the ideal family stolen that happiness?

Shouldn't they have gotten closer through their efforts to have a child? They'd seemed to be backing away from each other since they'd begun the quest to have a baby. Did Carrie feel inadequate because she couldn't give him a child? Had he somehow reinforced that feeling in her?

Brian heard footsteps in the hall. When Derrick appeared at the door, Brian closed the portfolio, zipped it and slipped it between the bookshelf and wall once more.

But the disturbing questions he'd asked couldn't be stowed away so easily.

Rain pelted Brian's windshield as he drove home from his office in the gathering dusk. Coming home was different now with Lisa in the house. A third person changed every dynamic. Yet even before Lisa had arrived, he and Carrie hadn't spent much time together. Except for their efforts to have a baby, they seemed to be living separate lives. Last night, when they'd made love, he'd still felt that separateness.

After Brian pulled into the garage and let himself into the kitchen, he listened. A hum of the TV came from Lisa's room. Would Carrie be with her? He decided to try to find his wife elsewhere in the house first. She often spent Sunday afternoons catching up on the phone with her sisters.

When he entered the foyer, he stopped. For convenience' sake, Carrie often dropped her purse on the marble-topped table there. Now he saw Lisa at the table, rifling through his wife's wallet. In fact she was slipping out a bill.

"What are you doing?" His voice was harsh and meant to startle the teenager.

Color drained from the girl's face. She was wearing one of the new sweat suits Carrie had bought her on their excursion to the mall, and she looked over at him now without the defiance she usually wore.

"I—I—" she stammered, dropping the wallet back into Carrie's purse, yet still holding a five-dollar bill.

"Where's Carrie?" he demanded.

"She—she went for a walk."

"So you took advantage of her absence to steal from her? Is there anything you've needed that we haven't provided for you?"

To Brian's surprise, tears welled up in Lisa's eyes and spilled over. He heard the sound of the French door closing in the family room, and a few moments later Carrie stood in the foyer eyeing them both. She was wearing a waterproof jacket, and she pushed the hood off of her head.

Seeing the tears on Lisa's face, she asked, "What's wrong?"

"Tell her, Lisa," Brian insisted.

"Mr. Summers saw me taking—taking money from your wallet. I'm sorry. I know I shouldn't, but..."

Carrie slipped off her gloves and stuffed them into one pocket. Going to Lisa, she asked, "Why do you need money?"

"I don't need it right now. I mean— I'm afraid of what's going to happen after I have the baby. What are you going to do with me? Do I have to leave right away? I still won't be able to afford an apartment. I can live on the streets again until I find a job, but—".

The tears were coming faster now and Brian saw a different side of Lisa Sanders—the vulnerable side. When the first tears had started to fall, he'd wondered if she was putting on an act. But now he saw the desperation in her eyes and he knew she wasn't. He'd been skating around this issue of Lisa, still angry with Carrie for making the decision of taking her in. But this girl was going to let them adopt her baby, and he had a responsibility for her. If she gave them her baby, it would be the most precious gift. She deserved to know she'd be taken care of. She deserved to know she could have a future different from her past.

Picking up the wallet, Carrie drew out a few bills and handed them to Lisa. "You don't have to worry about a place to stay after the baby's born. We're not going to put you out on the streets."

Lisa glanced over at Brian as if she didn't believe Carrie.

"We're not," he agreed. "Have you given any more thought to college?"

She wiped her tears away. "No, I didn't think you were serious. I thought you were just saying that so I'd give you the baby."

As he should have realized, Lisa didn't trust easily. His attitude toward having her in the house hadn't helped. "I don't make an offer like that then retract it. Why don't you come into my office and we'll take a look at a few colleges on the Internet. You can get an idea of what their programs are and what might interest you."

"I used the computer a few times at school, but I wasn't very good at it."

"I'll help you." After all, he still didn't trust her completely and he didn't want her alone in his office.

Lisa looked down at the bills in her hand and then thrust them back at Carrie. "I don't need this. You're taking care of everything I need."

"You should have your own spending money," Carrie said softly. "It was insensitive of us not to realize that."

"Carrie and I'll talk about it and we'll set up some type of allowance."

Lisa gave them a weak smile. "I haven't had an allowance since my parents died." Then before either of them could comment, she said, "I'll go look at that computer in your office."

After Lisa went down the hall, Brian stated, "We have to talk about Lisa, but I don't want to leave her alone in there."

Raindrops dripped from Carrie's jacket. After she unzipped it, she hung it across the foyer chair. "We should have talked after she arrived."

The anger he'd kept in check ever since Lisa had moved into their home came to the surface. "I didn't see much point in talking then. You made a decision without any input from me, and I was going to let you deal with it."

"I knew how much you wanted a child. I was just taking advantage of an opportunity."

"How much *I* want a child? Don't you want a child, Carrie?"

Lowering her head for a few moments, she finally met his gaze again. "Yes. But not to the exclusion of all else. Ever since the first year we were married, it's all we've been striving for."

"Is there something wrong with that?"

She looked suddenly defeated. "No. Not if it's what we both want. I guess I don't understand why you're angry about Lisa when *you've* been making all the decisions ever since we were married."

Her words took the wind from his logic. "I made all our decisions because I felt that's what you wanted. Are you telling me now I was wrong?"

When she took a deep breath and seemed to be sorting through the words she wanted to use, he became impatient. "Just say whatever you have to say, Carrie."

Squaring her shoulders, she did. "I'm not sure I knew what I wanted when we got married. Yes, I wanted to be married to you, but I didn't want a role like my mother had. She'd taken over everything—from having food on the table, to paying what bills she could, to taking care of us. So I guess after our wedding I just stood back, watching. You handled everything. I stopped modeling to be able to travel with you, to hostess dinner parties, to do volunteer work like the wives of the men you knew."

"Are you telling me you're sorry you stopped modeling?"

"I'm telling you I feel as if I don't have anything of my own anymore. I'm your wife, and I'm not sure who I've become outside of that."

"Is this an identity crisis?" he asked incredulously.

"I'm not sure what it is. Maybe I'm finally waking up and I want more."

"More? More than a house in a prestigious neighborhood, more than diamonds and furs and an unlimited bank account?"

With a frustrated frown, she waved her hand, dismissing everything he'd mentioned. "I'm not talking about things, Brian. The idea of adopting Lisa's baby means everything to me. A child would fill our lives the way nothing else can. But I worry if you're going to be around, or if you're going to be a ghost in and out of the baby's life."

"You believe since I haven't welcomed Lisa with open arms, I won't be invested in our baby?" The fact that Carrie thought that unsettled him. In his mind, one had nothing to do with the other. "I can't believe that you don't know me better than that. If we adopt a child, I'll take full responsibility for it."

"Responsibility is one thing. Caring and bonding and being with a child are another."

"Do you trust me, Carrie?"

Her brown eyes darted away from his. "Trust is complicated. It's not black and white."

He took her by the shoulders. "With me, it is. We've been married five years. By now you should know. I keep my promises, and I do what I say I'm going to do."

Suddenly her gaze met his and she asked softly, "Do you trust *me*, Brian?"

The question startled him, maybe as much as his had startled her. But he didn't have to think about it long. "I trust you to be faithful. I trust you to stand beside me. I trust you to tell me the truth. Yes, I trust you."

"But deep down, do you trust that I'll stay? Or do you keep yourself so busy with work that you'll be prepared if I leave?"

Brian couldn't remember ever being speechless in his life, but he felt as if Carrie's question had knocked the air from his chest. Considering her question and looking at the issues in his marriage he'd never even known were there unnerved him more than he wanted to admit. He relied on anger to fuel his response. "Did you bring this up now because you know we can't talk about it?"

"We can—"

"We can't. You brought a teenager into this house whom I caught trying to steal money from your purse. Do you think I'm going to trust her alone in my office?"

"Lisa was just afraid."

"Fear doesn't absolve her."

Carrie took a step back from him and he didn't like

that any more than he liked their discussion. "No, it doesn't," she murmured. "But stealing money for survival is a lot different from stealing for the kick of it. I don't think you have to worry about anything in your office."

His wife's tone had gone flat and Brian couldn't understand why his distrust of Lisa bothered her so much. Or was it something else he'd said? Carrie wasn't the type of person to let words wash over her and slide away. She remembered every one of them.

"We'll talk after I finish helping Lisa," he said, frustrated now.

"It will be time for dinner then. I invited Katie Crosby to come over. I have a pot roast in the oven."

"Verna didn't leave a casserole?"

"I told her I'd make dinner myself today. Lisa said pot roast is her favorite meal so it seemed like a good idea."

They hadn't discussed dinner, and he realized now that Carrie hadn't known if he'd be home. But she'd wanted to cook for her and Lisa and Katie, her best friend. Were there nights when she wanted to cook for him? When having a housekeeper didn't necessarily make things easy but made them impersonal?

The desire he felt for Carrie had always been powerful and he'd always felt it reciprocated. But right now he felt a wall between them, too difficult to climb, too thick to crash through. "We'll talk later."

When Carrie nodded, he saw the worry in her eyes and something more...something deeper that bothered him even more than her questions.

When he started to his office, he wasn't at all sure what later would bring. That troubled him most of all.

Seven

When the doorbell rang, Carrie hurried to answer it, glad Katie had arrived. She didn't know what had happened to her over the past week. She couldn't believe the honesty that came out of her mouth when she was talking to Brian lately. Befriending Lisa and the idea that she and Brian might actually have a child had given her more courage than she'd ever possessed. Was it courage...or recklessness? Courage...or the foolhardiness of wanting to spill everything about her life to Brian?

She knew she couldn't do that yet, not now with all this tension between them. He'd made it clear he thought right was right and wrong was wrong. He'd made it clear that nothing absolved a mistake. How could she ever tell him about the abortion, knowing it would probably destroy their marriage?

Opening the door to Katie, she was stunned by the

changes she saw in her friend. They'd met each other about three years ago at a local health club. Katie had just started a minimal exercise regimen. Back then she'd been overweight, had dressed inconspicuously and had worn glasses. She'd always let her brown hair fall long and straight, and it had hidden her face. Over the past few months, Katie had finally dropped quite a few pounds. However recently, Carrie had noticed other changes in her friend besides the weight she'd lost. She hadn't seen her since December, though, when she'd loaned her a dress for the bachelor auction and charity ball. Then Katie had gone down another dress size and hadn't had time to shop. In Carrie's closet they'd found an emerald sequined gown that had fit perfectly. Today her glasses were gone, and her hair was short and wispy around her face. Her black leggings and tall boots were topped by a hunter-green jacket.

"You look wonderful!" Carrie exclaimed before she could stop herself.

Katie gave her a shy smile. "You think so? This is the new me. I'm still trying to get used to her."

"Come on in."

After Katie came inside and unzipped her jacket, Carrie could see she wore a green cashmere sweater underneath that hugged her new figure.

"You know, if I'd seen you out on the street, I don't think I would have recognized you."

Looking away for a moment, Katie folded her jacket over her arm. "I've had that reaction before," she murmured.

Carrie wondered what was causing the sadness in her voice. Although Carrie loved her sisters dearly, she'd been the oldest and more like a second mother. Katie had become a good friend because they were around the same age with concerns they could share.

Taking her friend's coat, she hung it in the foyer closet. "Dinner will be ready shortly."

"Will Brian be joining us?"

"Yes. And we have a houseguest."

Katie looked taken aback. "Oh, I didn't know you were having company."

Her friend had always been shy and reserved, and Carrie tried to put her at ease. "Lisa's not exactly company. She's an unwed mother who's staying with us until she delivers her baby. Brian and I are hoping to adopt."

"That's terrific! When is she due?"

"Soon." Carrie hooked her arm through her friend's and guided her into the living room. "Can you believe I might become an instant mother?"

Sitting on the sofa, the two women grinned at each other. "After all the waiting and all the procedures, you're going to be a great mom. I can see you're obviously excited. Is Brian as thrilled as you are?"

Although she and Katie were close, Carrie had never told her about the rape or the abortion. But Katie did know how much she wanted a baby and how much Brian wanted a family.

Carrie felt as if she needed someone to talk to about all of this. "I'm not sure how Brian feels. Sometimes I think he's excited, but then others… I think he wants his *own* child. I'm so afraid he won't be able to accept this baby if we adopt him, that he'll think I let him down and we'll never have the perfect family he's always wanted because of me."

Katie's expression turned somber. "Have you talked to him about your concerns?"

"In a way. But I'm not always sure Brian knows what he's feeling, or will admit it."

"Did you go through an agency?"

"Yes, through Children's Connection."

"Did any of this come up during the interviews?"

"The questions came up and Brian answered them to the caseworker's satisfaction. He said he can accept an infant as his own. But he's having trouble accepting Lisa."

"Trouble?"

"She's…different. She's homeless, and she can be defiant sometimes. I think Brian just wanted someone to put a baby into our arms and then he could pretend the baby was his. I think he's having trouble with Lisa because she reminds him this infant won't be our biological child."

"Oh, Carrie." Katie's voice was sympathetic.

Brushing her hair behind her ear, Carrie shook her head. "I'm sorry. I didn't mean to lay this on you."

Katie clasped Carrie's hand. "We're friends. You can talk to me whenever you want."

"Thanks." After taking a deep breath and shoving her problems aside, Carrie suggested, "Let's talk about you. How were your holidays? With this new look, they must have been busy and exciting. Did you wear the dress you borrowed to the bachelor auction and ball?" The emerald-green dress was one of a kind. The designer's trademark was evident in the scalloped hem with its distinctive embroidery. The fashion designer had given it to Carrie on her very last modeling assignment. Brian had always liked the dress and kept a picture on his desk of her wearing it.

"I wore it," Katie said without elaboration.

"How was the event? Brian and I had another commitment that night but I would have liked to have gone. I heard Jenny Hall won a date with Eric Logan. Or shouldn't I mention the Logan name?" The Crosbys and Logans' long-standing feud often fueled gossip in the social circles around Portland.

Looking down at her hands in her lap, Katie said, "I hear Jenny and Eric are very happy, that their date led to a lot more and they're engaged. But you're right, I'd rather not talk about the Logans."

Carrie noticed Katie twisting her hands nervously. The Logans no doubt brought up bad memories for her friend. Katie had been a baby when Robbie Logan had been kidnapped, but she'd grown up in the Crosby family with the repercussions of it. However, Carrie thought Katie had gone on with her own life and put most of that in the past.

A little too quickly, Katie offered, "I spoke to Danny last week. He said you and Brian might take a trip to Hawaii."

Carrie remembered Ted and Brian talking about the possibility of asking Danny to be a reference for their Hawaiian deal. "Maybe Brian will be taking a trip to Hawaii, but I won't. I don't feel I should leave Lisa. Once her baby's born—*our* baby—I won't want to go anywhere."

So intent on her conversation with her friend, Carrie hadn't been aware of Brian and Lisa coming into the room. Brian's deep voice was gruff. "Hawaii's still up in the air. I didn't know you'd made up your mind about it, Carrie."

"I've thought about it a lot," she admitted, meeting his gaze. "Traveling with you this time just doesn't seem right."

She could almost hear what he was thinking—a lot of things between them now didn't seem right.

Addressing Lisa, Katie tried to diffuse the tension in the air. "I'm Katie Crosby. It's nice to meet you."

"You, too," Lisa said, lowering herself into an armchair. "You're as pretty as Carrie. Were you a model, too?"

Katie laughed. "Afraid not. I work in research and development with Crosby Systems."

"She's being modest." Carrie tore her eyes from her husband's and explained to Lisa, "She's a vice president."

"Wow! What did you take in college?"

Relieved when the conversation moved in the direction of what colleges Lisa might be interested in, Carrie excused herself to get dinner ready to put on the table.

Although Brian spoke with Katie and Lisa, he didn't seem to have much to say to Carrie during dinner. She tried to pretend nothing was wrong, but she was having a hard time. Her friend wasn't fooled by polite conversation that revolved in large around her sister Ivy, who had married a prince and become queen of Lantanya. The royal couple would be having a baby in April.

Lisa was fascinated by the fairy-tale story and she got along well with Katie. Carrie knew she shouldn't be surprised. Katie was a compassionate woman. She patiently answered Lisa's questions about Ivy, college and her work at Crosby Systems.

After dinner, Carrie quickly loaded the dishwasher and joined everyone in the living room. When she did, Brian excused himself to work in his office.

The women soon found themselves talking about fashions and clothes Katie had bought for her new image. She produced a picture and showed Lisa what she used to look like.

"I never knew anybody who had a makeover," Lisa said.

Katie laughed. "Well, now you do."

Finally Katie admitted she had to be going. "I have an early day tomorrow."

As Lisa went to her room, Carrie walked her friend to the door.

When Katie gave her a hug, she was encouraging. "Everything will work out with Brian and Lisa. You'll see. If you need to talk, give me a call."

Carrie gave Katie a tight squeeze. "Thanks. I'll do that."

A few minutes later, Katie had gone and Carrie stopped at Lisa's bedroom to say good-night. The teenager smiled at her. "I like your friend. She's cool."

"I like her, too. I guess that's why we're friends."

"Vice president of a company. That's really something."

"Do you want to be vice president of a company? You could. Business management is offered at a lot of colleges."

"Yeah, I saw that. Mr. Summers was a big help showing me how to get around the sites."

"I'm glad he could help you."

"He showed me how to download applications. I'm going to list this address as my home address."

She said it almost hesitantly, and Carrie realized Lisa still wasn't sure they'd let her stay even after the baby was born. "That's fine. This is where you'll be." Carrie suddenly had an idea that would involve Lisa more in their lives as well as in the community.

"I'm emceeing a telethon to encourage people to register for bone marrow transplants."

"That's where they donate their bone marrow, right? And then it's given to somebody else?"

"Right. People are going to call in and sign up and then later someone from the hospital will follow up with anyone who telephones. How would you like to man one of the phone lines?"

"Me? You'd let me do that?"

"Sure. I think you're responsible enough to take down all the necessary information. You'll get a chance to see the TV studio and get out for a bit. What do you think?"

"I don't know. I guess I can't wear jeans."

Carrie smiled. "We did buy that one dressier outfit. It'd be perfect."

"When is the telethon?"

"Tuesday evening."

"It's not like my social calendar's full or anything," Lisa muttered. After another moment's thought, she said, "All right. I'll do it."

"Great! I'll sign you up. You get a good night's sleep, and I'll see you at breakfast."

After Carrie closed the door to Lisa's room, she went to Brian's office. His door was slightly ajar and she could hear him talking on the phone. She'd wait for him upstairs no matter how late it was when he came up.

Carrie had been reading for about an hour when Brian entered the bedroom. He was wearing a red-and-black Henley shirt today and black jeans. His hair was mussed as if he'd run his hand through it a few times.

"I stopped at your office after I said good-night to Lisa, but you were on the phone."

"A call to Japan," he said absently. Then, looking at her in her nightgown, he suddenly suggested, "Let's get into the hot tub."

"The hot tub?" She couldn't remember the last time they'd gotten in together. Once in a while in the evening she took a long soak. Now and then, after his exercise regimen in the mornings, Brian would get in for a short amount of time. He didn't like to relax there as she did with music playing in the background.

"It's getting late," she said softly.

"Does it matter?" His question was almost a challenge.

Rising to her feet, she thought the hot tub might be a good place to talk—no interruptions, no phones ringing, just the two of them in the gazebo in the middle of the winter night.

Crossing to the closet, she said, "I'll change into my bathing suit."

"Just wear a robe."

Her gaze met his and a thrill of excitement rushed through her. Maybe he intended for both of them to simply be comfortable. Maybe he intended more. But with Lisa in the house...

As if reading her thoughts, he assured her, "Lisa's tucked into her bedroom for the night. After what happened with the alarm last time, I don't think she'll venture outside."

He was right about that. Suddenly the idea of being in the hot tub naked with her husband unnerved Carrie. They had things to discuss, they had their relationship to talk about. Maybe, Carrie hoped, that would lead to an intimacy they never had before.

A few minutes later, Carrie had wrapped herself in a long, fluffy yellow terry-cloth robe and slipped into sandals. Brian's robe was a navy-and-wine geometric design she'd bought him one Christmas. She wasn't sure he'd ever worn it before. He didn't bother with shoes.

When he let her precede him down the stairs, she felt a bit breathless. Her hand went to her hair. She'd used a scrunchie and fashioned it into a high ponytail. She'd also worn no makeup and now she wished she'd at least added a touch of lipstick.

The walk from the stairway through the family room seemed endless. Brian opened the doors onto the flagstone patio and they stepped outside.

"Your feet are going to get cold," she said inanely as they crossed the patio to a short, curved concrete path that led to the gazebo-shaped hot tub enclosure.

"They'll warm up fast enough in the hot water." His gaze met hers.

It was a cold January night, and it seemed to warm up more than a January night should. She hardly noticed the stars or the sliver of moon in the sky that was huge and black and enveloping in spite of the outdoor lights.

After Brian opened the door to the hot tub house and flipped the switch on the wall, he set the jets on the hot tub on low. There were blue lights set in the floor around the perimeter of the gazebo and now he switched those on, too.

Carrie stopped by a small redwood bench, sat on it, and removed her sandals while Brian uncovered the tub, set the cover aside and switched on the interior hot tub lights. Steam rose into the enclosed space, and he opened two of the jalousie windows to let the cooler night air in. As Carrie prepared to drop her robe, steam billowed from the tub and swirls of white wisps bathed the gazebo in almost otherworldly light. After Brian dropped his robe onto a redwood chair, he waited for Carrie at the steps, then offered her his hand.

He almost took her breath away. He was a magnificent-looking man. His shoulders were broad, the muscles in his upper arms defined. Curling light brown hair matted his chest from his throat to his navel. Carrie's breath became more shallow and she decided to forgo further appraisal of him. She would be too obvious. He would know what she was thinking. Wouldn't he?

That was what this was all about tonight—learning what the other was thinking, finding something they'd lost, reaching for something new.

Taking his hand, she climbed the two steps. Brian joined her and waited. She eased herself down onto the lip of the tub, then onto the seat. With room for six people, the hot tub almost felt like a small swimming pool.

However, as Brian lowered himself into the water beside her on the bench seat, he seemed to fill up the tub. Cool air became nonexistent, and she was lost in the swirl of mist as she watched her husband's face. She didn't know where to start with him, and she wondered now how they could have grown apart so much. Wanting to have a child should have brought them closer together. But she'd become lost in her guilt, and he'd become intent on his determination. Their paths had veered away from each other.

Needing to put words between them, needing to find a thread they could weave into something meaningful, she grasped the first topic that popped into her head. "Katie looks wonderful, doesn't she?"

"Yes, she does. Did she say why she suddenly made herself over?"

"Not really. She didn't seem to want to talk about herself except for her job. In fact, I thought she seemed a bit distracted."

"You didn't ask why?"

"I didn't feel I should pry. She'll tell me whatever it is when she's ready."

There had been a few inches separating them on the

bench, but now Brian moved closer to Carrie, stretched his arm out behind her and entwined one of his fingers around the hair of her ponytail. "I don't want to talk about Katie."

Tipping her head back, she looked up into his intense dark eyes. The blue glow of the perimeter lights faded into the yellow light emanating from the bottom of the tub. The mist between them seemed to float away or else it evaporated in the electric current zapping between them.

"What do you want to talk about?" she whispered, thinking about things like trust, time together, a new baby.

Untangling his fingers from her hair, he bent closer to her. "Maybe I don't want to talk at all."

Before she could protest that they had to, his fingers went to the scrunchie in her hair. "Mind if your hair gets wet?"

She was so torn between knowing she should force the conversation between them and just living in this moment with Brian. This was something they hadn't done for a very long time. She wanted him as much as he wanted her. Yet the wanting wasn't enough, was it? Hadn't the past year shown both of them that? Hadn't Lisa's presence and the idea of adopting a baby magnified the rift between them?

Her answer now and the way she responded to all of this would set the course of their future. Except for the very first night when she'd feared intimacy with Brian might resurrect flashbacks or take her back to a place she'd fought to get clear of, she'd never hesitated to let him awaken her desire. Even that first night her fears had been unfounded because the counseling had helped her clear her decks and she'd been ready for the gentleness, tenderness and passion that had gone along with Brian's love. She knew tonight she needed to welcome that passion again.

Afterward they could talk.

"I don't mind if my hair gets wet," she assured him.

Brian's slow smile made her pulse race unchecked. Taking the scrunchie from her hair, he set it on the lip of the tub. When he slid his hand up the back of her neck and shook out her long chestnut waves, she could tell he took pleasure from it.

"Come here," he whispered, and he brought her close—a breath's distance away. "It's been too long," he murmured as he brushed his thumb over her lips.

It did feel like forever since they'd made love, since he'd held her, since they'd lost themselves in each other. There was no need to speak as he first nibbled at the corner of her lips then bathed them with his tongue.

She clasped his shoulders, dizzy with desire, afraid she'd float away from him.

As he kissed first her upper lip, then her lower lip, teasing her unmercifully, she felt her breath come in short gasps. She wanted to beg him to do more, but she couldn't find her voice and she didn't want him to stop what he was doing. As if sensing that her need for his touch was increasing, his hand slipped under the water to caress her breast. When he fingered her nipple, she moaned. The whirl of the water against her skin, the mist swelling around them, the heat and cold mixing in the air awakened all of her senses until touch was the most acute of all.

His large hands caressed her everywhere, from her nipples to her waist to the most intimate place of all. He seemed intent on giving her so much pleasure that she was mindless with it, breathless with it, ecstatic with it. She didn't know how long he teased and tasted, nipped her shoulders while he touched, savored each kiss as if she was the nectar that could give him life. When his hand slipped between her thighs once more, she couldn't think clearly enough to do anything except arch against him. Water enhanced the slide of his fingers into the intimate heart of her. Soon every tingle in her body was coalescing into a tightening in her womb.

Brian knew exactly where to brush, where to stroke, where to linger until his thumb found the nub that brought on her climax. He kissed her again at the same time, and the cry of pleasure and release was lost into his mouth, into his body. The resonance of it seemed to vibrate through them both and before she could recover, he was sliding onto the reclining bench, pulling her onto his lap, looking into her eyes. His hands were on her hips, and she seemed weightless in the water. Splaying his hands across her backside, he lifted her onto him. As Brian filled her, Carrie braced herself on his chest and closed her eyes.

"This is going to be better than anything you've ever felt before," he promised her.

Brian always kept his promises.

The buoyancy of the water seemed to make everything light, everything easy, everything smooth. Each of Brian's thrusts became a pleasure-filled journey that took her deeper into their passion. She felt as if she were flying, soaring into another dimension as another climax started to build. The water, the heat, the feel of Brian's skin, the fullness of him inside of her flowed through her and around her and in her in increasingly engulfing waves. The waves gathered strength, each more explosive than the one before it until she couldn't tell where one wave stopped and another began…until she couldn't tell where she stopped and Brian began…until nothing mattered but riding the giant wave wherever it would take her.

Suddenly the crest broke into a thousand waves, each caressing her, each filling her, each shaking her with force. She held on to her husband for dear life. When she cried his name, it echoed in the mist, sounded on the redwood and became a prayer for everything she'd ever needed and wanted from him. She was trembling from the power of the orgasm when Brian's release came, too. He shuddered under her hands, enfolded her in his arms and brought her close into his chest.

This was exactly where she wanted to be—close to Brian, united with him. Yet she wasn't sure they were united, not emotionally. They had so much to talk about.

"We're going to overheat if we stay in here," he said with a satisfied smile a few minutes later. "Let's go back to our bedroom."

When she didn't respond right away, he asked, "Carrie? Don't you want to go to the bedroom?"

"I'd like to talk."

Kissing her forehead, he lifted her from him, then stood. "Talk? Wouldn't you rather finish what we started here?" He cupped her chin in his hand and his voice went husky and low. "This is what it's all about."

His words saddened her, disappointed her and made her ache for so much more. "I don't think that's true. Earlier you were upset because I started a conversation we couldn't finish. We need to finish it. I need to know if you trust me to stay and not leave, if you work so much because you don't want to get too close."

"We can't get closer than we were just now."

Steam billowed around Brian, making him appear as if he were a Roman hero emerging from the mist. Maybe that was the problem. She wanted a fairy tale, and she was faced with reality.

"I think our physical attraction has always gotten in the way of us getting close emotionally," she murmured.

After a frustrated groan, he shook his head. "I don't understand where all this is coming from. You're trying to psychoanalyze something that isn't there. Of course, I trust you to stay. You're nothing like Jackie Dennehy *or* my mother. You and I have built a life. We're finally going to have a family. My work is just that—my work. You had a career once. You know how it becomes the center of your life."

As the water swirled around her, she looked up at her husband. "I gave up my career because *you* became the center of my life."

His tone was disbelieving. "Do you resent that now?"

"No, I don't resent it. I'm trying to make a point. I want to know why you can't make room for me and a baby. Why can't we become the center of *your* life?"

"You're talking nonsense. Sure, I could retire, but then what? A man needs a worthwhile occupation. I'm good at what I do, Carrie. The problem is, it's not a nine-to-five job. You knew that when you married me."

"Yes, I knew that. But I didn't expect it to be a twenty-four-hour-a-day job, either. I didn't expect you to use it to keep up defenses, to stay removed from our marriage."

Raking his hand through his hair, he shook his head. "We're finally going to have what we've always wanted and you're starting arguments. I don't get it."

"I don't *want* to argue. I want to discuss. I want to compromise. I want us to trust each other with more than superficial details of everyday life. I don't want to be a single mom while you're a father in name only."

"If you're worried about how much time a child will take, you can hire a nanny."

"I don't *want* to hire a nanny!" She didn't think she'd ever raised her voice to him before but now she couldn't help it.

As she stood, she was almost trembling with the power of the yearning inside of her. "I don't want to live in a mansion with huge rooms that can never be filled. I want to live in a home, ringing with children's laughter. I want to bake cookies and watch you roughhouse with our son. I want us to put him to bed together and feed him in the morning. Don't you see what a real family can be?"

"Maybe I should rent reruns from the fifties to figure it out. I'll tell you right now 'Father Knows Best' wasn't real life then and it's not real life now." With a sigh, he stepped out of the tub. "Why don't you go on up and get a shower. I'll close up out here."

She was so frustrated, she could scream. She couldn't even suggest couples' counseling because in counseling, she'd have to be totally honest with him, totally open, totally naked. He wasn't ready for that any more than she was.

He was already closing the windows when she climbed out, put on her robe and belted it. She had to figure out some way to get through to Brian. Maybe a good night's sleep would help.

One look at his rigid stance told her he wouldn't be initiating more lovemaking tonight.

Neither would she. Until they could both shatter the barriers between them, chemistry would be all they had. It simply wasn't enough.

Eight

Checking her makeup in the downstairs bathroom, Carrie tried to still the butterflies fluttering in her stomach on Tuesday evening. The blush on her cheeks was rosier than she normally used, but it would look good under the lights.

Lights, cameras, microphones. It had been a long time since she'd been a spokeswoman for anything. She had to win over an audience tonight for the sake of the donor registry. At least thoughts of that challenge had helped her overcome her sadness and worry over her argument with Brian Sunday night.

When Carrie heard the garage door open, she gave a start. Brian. He'd left this morning before she was up. There had been a note for her on the refrigerator.

Carrie—I'll be home in time to take you to the studio. B.

When Brian came into the kitchen, he was carrying his briefcase and a newspaper under his arm. He looked at her as if he didn't know what to say for a moment and then obviously decided saying nothing about the two of them was best.

He held out the paper to her. "Have you seen this?"

Opening the *Portland Weekly,* a local tabloid, Carrie studied the section Brian mentioned. Her eyes opened in surprise. It was a picture of Peter Logan kissing a woman in what looked like a garden. The headline read, *Peter Logan Romances Mystery Woman.* The woman was in shadow, but Carrie recognized the hemline of the emerald dress she wore with its scalloped hem and intricate embroidery.

"I recognized that dress," Brian said. "No wonder Katie seemed distracted."

"I can't believe this! Not Katie and Peter Logan. Their families don't talk—they're still enemies."

Brian shrugged. "I know pictures don't always tell the whole story, but Peter and Katie look pretty friendly there."

"I wonder why they didn't publish the photo right after the bachelor auction."

"Whoever took it probably didn't realize what they had until they got the pictures developed."

"And then they sold one to the tabloid," Carrie agreed, concerned for her friend. "Do you think the *Weekly* will find out the woman is Katie?"

"I'll bet they've got someone on it now."

When Carrie heard footsteps, she turned to see Lisa coming through the doorway. She almost didn't know the girl. "Lisa, don't you look pretty!"

Lisa's hair was no longer two-toned, but all blond

now. In place of the garish makeup, she wore lipstick in a natural shade she must have purchased on their excursion to the mall. She was wearing the outfit Carrie had suggested would look nice, and the long-sleeved navy-and-red top covered her tattoos.

"The red was only wash-in hair color," she said, a defiant sparkle back in her eyes.

Brian studied Lisa until he broke into a smile. "You look incredible."

At that, the teenager blushed. "I figured the cameras might pan across the phones. They do that sometimes, don't they?"

"They sure do," Carrie answered with a smile of her own.

"Yeah, well, I didn't want to stand out. Are we leaving soon?"

Brian cast a questioning glance at Carrie.

"I'm ready. I want to call Katie but I'll do that later. I don't want to rush the conversation." Worried about her friend, Carrie knew Katie hated attention of any kind. If her identity was found out, she'd be mortified.

A half hour later when Carrie, Brian and Lisa arrived at the TV studio, Brian spotted Adam Bartlett immediately. The two men discussed clearing the trees on Cedar Run Ranch on Thursday.

Ever since Adam had donated his bone marrow to his half brother, he and Leigh had been actively involved in the donor registration program. Carrie saw Leigh organizing the phone volunteers and she introduced Lisa to her.

Once Lisa had been assigned a chair and a phone, she said to Carrie, "I know you probably have to get ready. Go ahead. I'll be fine."

Carrie affectionately touched Lisa's arm. "I know you will be, and you really do look wonderful tonight."

"If I intend to go to college and eventually become a vice president of something, I figured I had to make certain adjustments. Besides, *you* always look like a million bucks and you hardly wear any makeup at all."

Carrie could see that the teenager was sincere. Apparently she was a role model for her, and she felt good about that. "I'll check in with you before the show starts. I have to meet and talk with the families I'm going to be interviewing. It will help us all relax when we finally do get started. If you need anything, just ask Leigh."

"Okay," Lisa agreed, then sat at her station.

Fifteen minutes later, Brian found Carrie in the green room with the families. He gave her a thumbs-up sign and told her he'd be in the audience. For a few moments, Carrie's thoughts wandered to the other night in the hot tub and their argument afterward. It was still floating between them, and she didn't know how to wipe it away.

As Brian took a seat in the audience and the ninety-minute program began, he watched Carrie, suddenly overtaken by the feeling that he didn't know her. That was ridiculous! Of course he knew her.

Then why hadn't he realized before now that their marriage was on rocky terrain? Why hadn't he seen red flags? In the past two weeks there had been enough of them to blind him—Carrie making a decision to bring Lisa into their house without consulting him, Carrie's eyes lighting up as she'd taken care of the teenager, Carrie caring for Lisa rather than rejoining their dinner party, Carrie telling him she didn't want to be a trophy wife, Carrie asking if he trusted her, Carrie saying she was happy *but*…

That "but" was monumental, filled with countless other things she hadn't said.

On the monitor, he saw Carrie's eyes become moist as she spoke to a mother and a young son who had had a bone marrow transplant. The little boy's hair still hadn't grown back, and there was so much compassion on Carrie's face, Brian knew every viewer had to feel it as much as he did. As she interviewed donors about their part in the life-saving procedure, as she drew from doctors their expert opinion about bone marrow transplants, as she made a plea to the viewing public to call and register for the donor program, Brian began to see his wife in a new light.

The hour-and-a-half program passed quickly. After it was over, he saw Carrie was deluged by a number of people who had something to say to her—thank you, congratulations, a warm goodbye. When he checked on Lisa, she was still compiling the forms she'd filled out when Portlanders had called in. Brian couldn't get over the changes in her since she'd washed the red out of her hair and eliminated the eyeshadow. She looked like any daughter a father might be proud of. With sudden clarity he realized Carrie had seen Lisa's good qualities before the transformation.

"How did it go?" he asked the teenager now.

As usual, her defenses were up. Her shoulders squared and she said, "It went fine."

"That was a long time to be taking phone messages," he said lightly as he noticed her rubbing her back.

"The time flew. I just hope I have everything filled in right."

"I'm sure you do. As long as you have a contact number, Leigh can do a follow-up if she has to."

Lisa looked down at the forms in her hand and finally met his eyes again. "I wanted to tell you, I mailed the college applications this morning that we downloaded from your computer."

"You did? How many?"

"Three—to UCLA, the University of Puget Sound in Tacoma and the University of Colorado at Boulder. Now we'll see if any of them accept me. I spent a long time on the essays."

"Did you keep copies? I'd like to read them."

"Carrie let me use the word processing program on her laptop. I have them saved on disk. I'll make sure you get a copy. Once I give these forms to Leigh, I'll be ready to go, but I think I'll try to find a ladies' room before we do."

"That's fine. Carrie's still on the set. I'll be there with her."

When Brian reached the stage set, he found Carrie talking to a man who looked familiar to him. The guy was in his forties with dark-brown hair, wearing a charcoal pinstriped suit, blue shirt and designer tie. When Carrie caught sight of Brian and introduced the two men, everything fell into place. Charles Gallagher was one of the producers at the TV station. Brian had seen him at Chamber of Commerce meetings.

The two men shook hands. Charles didn't hesitate to tell Brian why he was talking to Carrie. "Your wife has a gift."

Brian wasn't exactly sure what the man meant so he kept quiet and waited.

Gallagher gave Carrie a wide smile. "She's very humble, but I can tell her interview skills rival anyone's, even Barbara Walters'!"

"I think you're exaggerating," Carrie said with a little laugh.

"I'm not exaggerating in the least. You made everything about this production look easy, and it wasn't, I know. Parents are emotional about their children, kids clam up, doctors talk in medicalese. You handled all of it brilliantly and that's why I want to meet with you about doing a talk show."

"A talk show?" Brian asked now. He could tell Carrie was comfortable with Gallagher and vice versa and he didn't know if he liked it. Gallagher seemed to have an extra sparkle in his eye whenever he looked at Carrie.

"Yes. The station is considering doing a live talk show every morning. We have the market for it. I want to talk details, but all your wife will say is that she'll take a meeting with me."

That surprised Brian. However, Carrie was doing lots of things lately that surprised him.

"Anyway," Gallagher said, taking Carrie's hand and squeezing it, "I'll see you on Thursday morning at nine. Don't get cold feet on me."

She smiled. "I won't."

After a nod to Brian, Gallagher left them on the empty set.

"The idea of a talk show just came up now?" Brian asked.

"Yes. Of course, I can't do it, not if we're going to have a baby. But…"

Brian knew Carrie was hoping for the best scenario—that Lisa would have her baby, give him up for adoption and then go off to college. But there were other possibilities, too.

"You want to be prepared if Lisa decides not to give up her baby."

"I don't know if prepared is the right word, but I learned a long time ago not to close doors. There's no harm in taking a meeting with Charles."

So they were on a first-name basis. "How long have you known Gallagher?"

"For years, actually. Before we were married, I organized a fashion show. He was the producer on the news then and taped it. We went to dinner a few times."

Brian suddenly went on alert. "You never told me that."

"Did you tell me about every woman you dated before we were married?"

"No, of course not."

"The old double standard?" she asked easily.

Ignoring that question, he commented, "You seemed comfortable with him. Were you involved?"

Carrie had seemed so inexperienced the first time they'd made love that he'd guessed there hadn't been many men in her life. He'd felt more than once that he'd been her first serious relationship.

"No, we weren't involved. We might have become good friends, though, but our lives took different directions. He concentrated on his career and I married you."

"Gallagher isn't married?"

"Let's just say he still hasn't found the right woman."

"Maybe he wishes he hadn't let you get away."

Her eyes widened, and Brian wondered if his suggestion was really that off the mark.

"And you think that's the reason he's offering me the talk show?"

"I don't know what his reasoning is."

"You don't believe he thinks I'm really talented?"

"I don't know his motives. I just know I don't like the way he looks at you. That gleam in his eye has nothing to do with whether or not you're a good interviewer."

"I guess I'll know after my meeting with him." There was a coolness in Carrie's voice that hadn't been there before.

"I'm not suggesting you don't take the meeting."

"What *are* you suggesting?"

"That you be careful when you do."

Her chin rose a notch and color marked her cheeks. "I haven't lived in a bubble since I married you, Brian. I've dealt with men on the hospital board, doing foundation work, not to mention all your colleagues and associates. I know who's safe and who isn't. I have built-in radar."

Something about the way she said that made him ask, "And where did that come from?"

She seemed to hesitate a moment, then she gave a little shrug. "I guess it came from knowing what some photographers were thinking when they looked through the camera lens when I posed for them. There were some I liked to work with and some I didn't. I appreciate your protective streak, but I really don't need it. I'm not eighteen, I'm twenty-seven, and I know self-defense."

Not much she could have said would have surprised him more. "When did you learn self-defense?"

Again there were a few moments of hesitation. Finally, she replied, "I took the first class when I was nineteen. Since then, I've taken a refresher course about once a year."

"And you didn't tell me?"

"It's just one of the things I do when you're gone, Brian, just like working out at the gym, yoga and flower arranging."

"Don't act as if we don't spend any time together. We do. If I don't know something about you, it's because you haven't told me."

Now his wife went paler. "If you check your daily planner for the past year, and you add up the time you think we spent together, I doubt if it would be as much as you believe."

Carrie's gaze veered away from his, and when it did, she caught sight of Lisa. Beckoning to the eighteen-year-old, she broke into a smile. "Leigh told me you did a great job of manning the phone. How are you feeling?"

"Like I could eat a hot fudge sundae—hot fudge over mint-chocolate-chip ice cream."

Though Brian was distracted by everything he and Carrie had talked about, he was developing a fondness for this teenager. "I know an ice cream shop that will still be open. One hot fudge sundae coming up."

When he glanced at Carrie, she avoided his gaze. While they were eating, maybe he could figure out which way to go with his wife. How to pull her closer instead of pushing her away. Somehow tonight the chasm between them had opened wider. He had to find a way to close it, and close it soon.

The following afternoon, as Brian took Exit 28 off of I-84, Carrie finally guessed where they were going. Brian hadn't left the house as early this morning as he usually did and when he'd had breakfast with her, he'd asked if she wanted to take a drive with him this afternoon. After their conversation last night at the TV station, she didn't know what he had planned. But now she knew they were headed for Bridal Veil Falls State Park. The area used to be a logging center, and large timber stands were everywhere. She remembered absolutely everything about this place. Bridal Veil Falls was where Brian had proposed to her.

After they exited the car, Brian suggested, "Let's take the upper trail."

That trail took visitors around the precipice and the cliffs of the Columbia River Gorge. It was an awesome sight even in the winter, or maybe especially in the winter. She and Brian hadn't talked much during their ride here. There was a tension between them now that never seemed to go away. Old boundaries between them seemed too restrictive but they hadn't formed new ones yet. Everything seemed to be changing.

She didn't know if that was good or bad.

It was definitely different.

When she thought again about making love with Brian in the hot tub the other night, she knew they could have so much more than they did have. Did Brian *want* more? Or did he want everything to stay the same? She had the feeling "same" was a thing of the past.

The trail was neatly fenced with beams and wire to protect onlookers. Every view of the gorge was spectacular. The scents of rock, firs and damp underbrush were strong, and she hiked beside Brian, often casting quick glances at him. Her husband was wearing a sheepskin jacket and jeans. Rain was common in January, but today a reflection of sun glowed out between the clouds.

They were the only ones on the viewing platform. Bridal Veil Falls was two-tiered. The water fell from the top of nearby Larch Mountain, over the cliffs and into the river. Carrie concentrated on the beautiful veil of water, remembering Brian's proposal. That day, before she'd accepted his offer of marriage, she should have told him everything. If he'd walked away then, she would have survived. If he walked away now—

"No land developer could create anything that would match this," Brian said in a low voice.

Brian wasn't the type of developer to put together a deal on a mall simply to make a profit. He believed in revering the natural setting as much as possible. They'd talked about that a lot when they'd first met, and she knew Brian was still committed to that concept.

She was turned toward the falls, away from him. Brian clasped her shoulder and nudged her around.

The wind tossed her hair and although she could have raised the hood on her parka, she didn't. Brian's gaze was too intent, too searching, and she felt paralyzed in the moment.

"I brought you here so we'd have some time together today, so we could talk—away from the city, away from Lisa, away from everything that seems to be dragging us down lately."

"It's beautiful here." Her heart was beating so fast, it was hard to catch her breath.

"*You're* beautiful," Brian murmured and took her face between his hands.

His skin was warm on her cheeks. There was desire in his eyes and something else, too…something much deeper. However, what he felt wasn't based on truth. She realized now she had projected an image to him. She'd become that image. She understood after all these years, she was fighting it, fighting to show him who she really was.

He brushed her nose with his, then kissed her. Out here in the midst of a river canyon, high-rising cliffs, Douglas firs and the sound of the falls rushing to the water below, she felt as if they were the only two people on earth. Brian took his time with the kiss, coaxing her into it, tempting her with his tongue, seducing her with his desire.

She was so close to heaven…yet so far away.

Her need to be everything that Brian ever wanted urged her to respond completely. Lacing her fingers in his hair, she let him take her where he always took her—outside of herself and into him.

Finally he tore himself from her, came back for another kiss, then leaned away and studied her. "I brought you here to tell you a couple of things."

Breathless, she began to convince herself that this was the moment, this was the time she should tell him about the rape, tell him about the abortion, tell him what she wanted for the two of them.

"First, I have to fly to Alaska the day after tomorrow."

Carrie closed her eyes. She couldn't look at her husband and let him see her disappointment.

"Carrie, it will only be for a few days. The Alaskan deal is at a crucial stage and I have to make the trip. For about twenty-four hours you won't be able to get in touch with me. There won't be any phones, and cell phones won't work."

"What if Lisa has her baby?"

"I'll only be out of touch for a day, I promise. Believe me, I want to be there when Lisa delivers her baby as much as you do. That's why I'm making this trip now instead of next week."

Struggling to keep tears from filling her eyes, she took a deep breath.

"Carrie, I can't not do this because Lisa *might* have her baby. Don't you understand that?"

She shook her head. "You say you want to be here as much as I do. I don't think that's true. If it were true, you wouldn't go out of town at all. Why can't you just wait?"

He didn't look angry, but his voice was firm. "I can't wait. Not on this trip. But I *am* going to send Ted to Hawaii instead of going myself. I'm going to give him more authority on the project and see how it goes. If he does a good job, I'll be able to cut back on traveling. That's what you want, isn't it?"

"It has to be what *you* want, too."

"I've always wanted a family. You know that. I've always seen us with kids in our lives, and I suppose I never truly realized what that would mean. You asked me if I want to be a real father. I *do.* But I can't cut back recklessly. I've worked hard to build Summers Development, and I want to make sure it's still strong even if I don't put in as many hours and take as many trips as I used to. I want it to be our child's legacy. Can you understand that?"

She understood change couldn't happen overnight. She understood that now wasn't the moment to turn herself inside out and expose everything she was to him. "I understand."

He stroked the back of his hand down her cheek. "Then why do you look so sad?"

Marshalling her emotions into a manageable lot, she tried for a smile. "I'm not sad, just concerned. If something happens with Lisa while you're gone..." *I'm afraid what will happen to us.*

"Nothing is going to happen to Lisa. Worst-case scenario, I'll miss the delivery. But the child will be ours in every way that matters, Carrie. I promise you that, too. Best-case scenario, I'll be back before this baby even thinks about coming into the world. Okay?"

What else could she say? "Okay."

The silence between them trembled with unspoken thoughts. Hesitantly she asked, "Are you still going to Adam and Leigh's ranch tomorrow?"

"I told him I'd help him cut down those trees and I will."

"I thought maybe since you took off this afternoon, you wouldn't have the time."

"This afternoon is ours. Let's just enjoy it. It has nothing to do with tomorrow."

Couldn't Brian see that everything was connected? Couldn't he see that she wasn't sure what meant the most to him? Couldn't he see that she was afraid?

When Brian turned toward the falls, he dropped his arm around her shoulders. She knew that he didn't see, and she felt more afraid than ever that she'd lose him.

Nine

It was 5:00 a.m.

Brian couldn't sleep. Careful not to wake Carrie, he left their bed, noiselessly slid into his jeans and went downstairs. Yesterday afternoon hadn't gone exactly as he'd planned. He'd thought their trip to Bridal Veil Falls would reconnect them. He'd thought telling Carrie he wasn't going to Hawaii would please her. But she'd focused on the Alaska trip and she'd known about that all along.

After they'd returned home, they'd had supper with Lisa, then Brian had worked in his office for a while, quit early and gone to the bedroom to find Carrie watching the news. Afterward they'd made love, yet he'd sensed both of them were guarded. Neither were giving everything they had, and he couldn't figure out what was going wrong.

In his office now, he didn't feel like working. That was a first. He found himself pulling a sketch pad from the closet. He'd put it there when they'd moved in.

Sitting at his drafting table, he took pencil in hand and let his subconscious guide his fingers. He'd been working for an hour when he finally leaned back and perused what he'd drawn. The falls were in the background, and he and Carrie were standing at the viewpoint gazing at each other. He was reaching out and touching her cheek. Sometimes he felt emotions so deep between the two of them, he didn't want to delve into them.

A question she'd asked haunted him. Did he keep himself so busy with work that he'd be prepared if she left?

He'd denied that was what was going on. Yet in the face of everything that was happening, and looking at it now, he wondered if Carrie's insight had been correct.

Placing the sketch he'd drawn inside the sketchbook, he returned it to the closet. Adam was expecting him today. The sheer physical labor might help him clear his head more than anything else could.

When Brian arrived at Adam's house and rang the doorbell, Leigh opened the door with a smile. A short time later, she handed her husband a Thermos and two mugs, kissed him and told him she'd be leaving for Portland General. She had a meeting with a few of the staff members who were considering giving some of their weekend time to the Kids Camp at Cedar Run, which was what they'd decided to call their endeavor.

Brian and Adam wasted no time as they examined the area Adam wanted to clear, gathered equipment and went to work. Dampness in the air and the low-slung gray clouds portended more rain. But for the time being, they were dry.

Brian had handled a chain saw during his lumberjack days after high school. He'd earned money any way he could, and he'd saved every cent he could for three years. He still remembered the satisfaction of buying that first property. Fortunately for him, it had doubled in value in two years and he'd been on his way. He'd done his research and gone into real estate knowing exactly what to look for. People skills had come next, and he'd learned the most important quality of all—patience. Never rush a client or a deal. That patience had paid off.

After the trees were felled and chopped into manageable sections, Adam and Brian sank down onto the thick logs and opened the Thermos of coffee.

Adam rotated his shoulder and moved his head from side to side. "I think I'm getting too old for this."

Brian laughed. "Or maybe we should do it more often."

"I have a feeling that chasing after the kids who come to the camp will keep me in good shape. I really can't wait till we get the place opened."

Besides seeing Adam's excitement, Brian had sensed the same anticipation in Leigh. "This could be a twenty-four-hour-a-day project. Are you and Leigh ready for that?"

With a nod, Adam rested his mug on his knee. "Yeah, we are. We've talked about it, and we want to make sure we have enough help so she and I can sneak away together at least one day a week. There will be lulls, too, probably. Sometimes we'll have lots of kids, others maybe only a few."

"As busy as you're going to be, have you and Leigh thought about having kids of your own?"

"Sure we have. And we're practicing already," Adam added with a grin. "I've learned everything happens in its right time. Suddenly I have more family than I ever expected to have. For years I felt as if I were alone, then barriers broke down with my adoptive family, I met my birth father and became a part of his brood. On top of all that, I learned I was a triplet. Now I feel as if I've known Lissa and Sam all my life and it's been less than a year. It all seemed to happen when it was supposed to happen—Leigh coming back into my life in the midst of all that included. So I guess I believe when we're supposed to have kids, we'll have them. If for some reason we can't make a baby, we'll have each other."

With blinding awareness, Brian realized he hadn't gone into marriage with that type of thinking. All those years he and his dad were alone, he'd wanted a family more than he'd wanted anything else. As a teenager, he'd known he would pick the right woman and eventually he'd have three or four kids running around. But now he wondered what his attitude and his dreams had cost him.

Had Carrie always felt that he wanted a family more than he'd wanted her? She'd reminded him that for most of their marriage, they'd been striving for kids. She'd wanted them, too, but had the striving made her feel insecure? And when she'd found out she couldn't get pregnant naturally, had she felt less than whole? Why hadn't she ever discussed it with him? Why did he feel there was always a piece of herself she wasn't giving him?

"Valentine's Day is coming up soon," Adam said with a wink.

Brian adjusted to the quick change of subject. "In a few weeks."

"I'm thinking about taking Leigh on a cruise to Ta-hiti. We might not get a chance for that anytime soon after Kids Camp opens."

A trip to Tahiti. He and Carrie might be spending their Valentine's Day with a newborn baby. The thought of it made him smile. But then he considered the last few Valentine's Days, going to dinner…*if* he wasn't out of town. He'd had his secretary order flowers. This year Carrie needed more than a token, more than a piece of jewelry, more than an expensive trinket, and he suddenly understood what could be the perfect gift. He'd spend more time on that sketch and have it framed for her. Maybe that would bring back the light in her eyes. Maybe that would show her he was as committed to her now as he had been on the day they married.

After the last swallow of coffee, he set the mug aside. "Okay. Let's get these logs split, then we can say we really had a workout."

Adam groaned and got to his feet. "This could take the rest of the day."

Brian didn't care. The physical labor *was* helping to clear his head. Maybe by the end of the day he'd have more than a present for Valentine's Day figured out.

Everett Baker sat at his desk at Children's Connection, his head in his hands. How had he gotten into this mess? How had he gotten involved in a black-market baby kidnapping ring and everything that went with it?

For the first time in his life, he'd decided to make a friend. The man known as the Stork had seemed so sincere, so sympathetic, so…friendly.

And then there were the flashbacks he was still having. At first he'd thought they were snippets of dreams of the family he'd always wanted to have rather than the weird one he'd been stuck with. But now he knew the visions were too real to be dreams; now he knew they were memories. Every time he was with Nancy, they came with more force. Because she was the kind of presence in his life he'd never had? Because she was so kind and caring he wanted to take her to bed, shut the door to her apartment and never open it again? Getting more deeply involved with Nancy would put her in harm's way. He knew it. That was the last thing he wanted to do.

The cell phone sitting on his desk rang. He glanced at the clock on the wall and knew who was calling. The Stork had said 3:00 p.m. and he was never late.

Picking up the phone, Everett answered resignedly, "Hello?" He wanted out, but he knew the Stork would never let him get out.

"Have you found any more rich couples who want to adopt?" the caller asked without preamble.

"I'm working on it." Truth be told, he wasn't trying very hard. Yesterday he'd heard about a couple with money that the adoption agency had turned down. They'd left after a very loud argument with their caseworker. If the Stork pushed him, he'd get in contact with them next week.

"I need to hear more enthusiasm here, Baker. You can't be the loose cog in my wheel."

"I know I can't. I may have another couple for you by the end of the month."

"*That's* what I like to hear, but it had better be sooner than later. I also wanted to remind you, I expect you to snatch the Sanders baby when the girl delivers."

Sweat broke out on Everett's brow. The Stork had

given him those orders a few weeks ago, but he just couldn't follow them.

"Look, I've been thinking. Taking a baby from the hospital is much different than taking one from an unwed mother living on the streets. Everyone at the hospital knows me. I'll stick out like a sore thumb. Besides that, I know nothing about babies. Couples were waiting for the others. What are we going to do with this kid till we find someone to pay for him?"

When the Stork stayed silent, Everett was afraid to breathe.

Finally the Stork admitted, "You've made some points." After a few more moments ticked by, he decided, "I'll find someone else to do it. You *are* too recognizable. My sister's husband has two jobs and they always need money. I'll drop the kid there till we find a couple. She has three of her own so she'll know what to do."

"That sounds like a plan," Everett agreed quickly, desperately relieved to be off the hook.

"You're not turning chicken on me, are you, Baker?" The Stork's voice held menace.

"Of course not," Everett lied, knowing the caller expected a definitive answer.

"That's good. Because if you ever consider it, remember, I'll have to tell Nurse Allen what you've been up to."

The Stork's mention of Nancy made chills ripple up Everett's spine. "Leave Nancy out of this," he snapped.

"I might leave her out of it if you do what I tell you to do. I want another couple soon, got it?"

"Got it," Everett mumbled. "I've got to go," he lied again. "Someone just knocked on my door."

"Keep the faith," the Stork warned in a singsong voice as he clicked off.

Everett stared at the cell phone, then with a burst of frustration and anger roiling up inside of him, he threw it across the room. It bounced off the wall and hit the tile floor with a thud. But it didn't fly into pieces, and Everett knew whether that phone was broken or not, the Stork would find a way to contact him.

Pushing away from the desk, he stood and paced, feeling sick inside, knowing he should cancel his date with Nancy tonight. She could always guess when something was wrong.

On the other hand...

He needed to see her because he didn't know how much longer he could keep her in his life.

When Brian returned from Cedar Run Ranch, Carrie was in the kitchen looking flushed and harried. There were two pots simmering on the stove and the oven timer buzzed.

"What's going on?" he asked.

Carrie held up her hand for him to wait a minute as she opened the oven door. After she pulled out a chocolate cake, deciding it was done just right, she set it on a rack on the counter.

"Lisa's having a friend over and I'm cooking. She's going to stay the night."

"Stay the night?"

Placing the pot holder on the counter, Carrie stepped closer to him. "Don't worry. It's only one night. I thought it would be fun for Lisa. The shelter's really full right now."

"Is it the girl she met at the mall for lunch?"

"Yes. Ariel Bridges. Will you be here for supper? I'll have it ready in about half an hour."

"Yes, I'll be here. I have to make a few calls later."

"About your trip to Alaska?"

"Yes." He could see in her eyes that she still didn't want him to go, but he felt she was worrying needlessly about Lisa. Her dismay about this trip was coming from more than that. "How did your meeting go with Gallagher?" He'd thought about her meeting with the man more than once today.

Avoiding his gaze, she went to the counter and began tossing lettuce in a teak bowl. "It went okay."

"Did he push you about the talk show?"

"I told him again that it was out of the question."

Her voice had a note in it that made Brian ask, "But?"

Facing him again, she replied, "He suggested something else. He suggested one segment a week where I would focus on Children's Connection as well as Portland General Hospital. They'd use it in the morning news and keep viewers informed as to what's happening there. Taping time would involve one or two days a week."

He could hear the underlying excitement in her voice. "What do you think about doing that?"

"If the adoption with Lisa goes through, I wouldn't. I want to be a stay-at-home mom. But if it doesn't…"

If the adoption didn't go through, this job would get her in the working world again. In fact, he was sure it would lead to more—maybe that talk show. A month ago he would have vetoed the whole idea, but now he knew he couldn't. He could see Carrie needed more in her life than traveling with him and being a hostess. He should have seen it sooner.

"You'll have to make the decision on this, Carrie, but

even as a mother, you could hire a nanny for two days a week. Working and having a baby aren't incompatible."

Her eyes widened at his comment, and he could see she was startled by it. He was, too. Their lives were definitely changing and it gave him an unsettled feeling. "Is there anything I should know about Ariel before I meet her? As in tongue piercings, purple hair…"

Carrie's smile was instantaneous. "Nope. In fact, I think you'll like her."

The heck of it was, he was beginning to like Lisa, too.

Carrie enjoyed dinner with the two girls and thought maybe Brian did, also. He listened more than joined in the conversation, but he asked questions every once in a while.

When Ariel told him about losing her job and apartment, he shook his head. "I can see how that can happen."

Carrie's gaze gravitated to Brian's now and then. When it did, the trip to Alaska stood between them. She realized he wanted to be reasonable about it but he couldn't just stay home and wait for Lisa to have her baby. Yet another part of her wished he would. She wished he'd put their marriage and their life first for a change.

When the phone rang, Brian said, "I'd better get that."

They were eating dessert then, and with the call, which Carrie suspected was about his trip, she knew she'd lose him for the evening.

However, when he answered, he didn't take the cordless phone to his office. He stood stock-still. "Yes, it *has* been a while. Five years."

Brian's stony expression told Carrie who the caller might be. There was only one person she knew of with whom he hadn't been in contact for five years—his mother.

Now Brian did move into the hall with the phone. Lisa and Ariel were forking in chocolate cake and talking about one of their other friends at the shelter. She heard Lisa say, "I'd really like to see everybody before I have this baby. I'm not exactly sure what will happen afterward."

"You have a home here, Lisa," Carrie reminded her again, knowing the teenager needed to hear it over and over so she'd believe it.

"I know, that's what you said. But after the baby's born, I'm not going to want to sit around all day, either. I thought I could get a job waitressing again to make money for college. I know Mr. Summers said he'd pay for it, but I'd like to have money of my own, too. You know what I mean?"

Carrie knew exactly what she meant. But before she could tell Lisa she'd help her find a job if that was what she wanted to do, Brian came back into the room. He was frowning and lines creased his brow. She didn't want him to shut her out.

"Who was it?" she asked.

His gaze collided with hers. "My mother."

"She lives in Portland?" Lisa asked. "You never mentioned her."

Carrie held her breath, not knowing how Brian would reply to the question. He didn't like talking about Muriel Summers. "No, she doesn't live in Portland. She's living in Montana."

"Montana. That's cool. On a ranch?"

Brian rubbed his forehead. "No, in Billings."

"You must love going there to visit her. I heard—"

"I don't visit her, Lisa. She left when I was seven and didn't get in contact with me till I made some money." Looking at Carrie, he said, "I'm going to my office."

"Mr. Summers?" Lisa asked.

Brian stopped.

"Does she want money from you now?"

One thing Carrie admired about Lisa was that she didn't back down when she wanted to know something. She didn't back away from the hard questions, either.

The rigidity in Brian's stance told Carrie how difficult this conversation was for him. "She says she doesn't want anything. Her husband died a few months ago and she'd like to visit."

"You don't want her to visit?"

"Why would I?" he asked as if asking himself. "First she went twenty-two years without a word to me, then five more years. Why should I want to see her now?"

Lisa's answer came swiftly. "Because she's your mom. I don't have one anymore and I wish I did."

As Brian focused on Lisa, his demeanor softened a bit. "It's not the same thing."

Then he went down the hall to his office and closed the door.

Carrie didn't usually bother Brian when he wanted to be alone. Tonight was different. She wanted to know what he was thinking and feeling, and there was only one way to do that.

"If you girls want another piece of chocolate cake, go right ahead. I'll be back in a few minutes."

At Brian's den, Carrie rapped lightly on the door but didn't wait for him to call to her. She opened it and went inside. He wasn't working or making phone calls. He was standing at the window looking out into the winter night.

She came up behind him and just stood there for a few moments.

Finally he said, "She's lonely. She doesn't have anyone left. She wants me to forgive her. How can I do that? She left and didn't look back."

"She's looking back now," Carrie offered softly. "Maybe she's always regretted leaving. Maybe she knows it was a mistake."

"She chose a different life. All right, so she fell in love with someone else. That didn't mean she had to pretend I never existed. Not one phone call, Carrie. Not one letter."

"Until we got married."

"Too little too late."

"You don't know what she was thinking. You don't know her side of it."

"She was tired of living with my father and his gambling. She found something better. That wasn't a mistake, Carrie; that was a choice. But never looking back for me was a choice I can't forgive."

Carrie's heart was beating fast and it ached. She'd made a choice, too. Brian would think her choice was as unforgivable as his mother's. She knew he liked the people in his life to be perfect, to meet his expectations. Like his mother, she wasn't perfect. If he knew that, he wouldn't want her.

"Maybe some mistakes *are* too big to forgive," she murmured. Her eyes swam with sudden tears, and he saw them.

"What's wrong?"

"I was just thinking about how your mom must be feeling." Her voice broke and all the things she wanted to tell Brian formed a rock in the pit of her stomach. "I'll let you make your calls," she mumbled as she turned to leave.

Brian caught her arm. "Carrie, are you all right?"

"Fine," she managed to say. "I want to make sure the girls are settled for the night then I'll go upstairs." Somehow she staved off the tears. Somehow she raised her gaze to him and kept her despair from him.

"I'll try not to be too late," he assured her.

Usually the night before he left on a trip, they made love. But tonight Carrie knew she couldn't do that. She couldn't make herself vulnerable with Brian. She couldn't pretend their marriage was strong when it wasn't. Tonight she'd be asleep when Brian came to bed. That was just the way it had to be.

Carrie pulled her fleece jacket from the foyer closet, wondering if she was doing the right thing, leaving Ariel and Lisa alone while she visited her family in Windsor. As she put on her jacket, she knew she would only be gone until dinnertime. Certainly Lisa and Ariel would be fine for a few hours.

Before Brian had left Portland yesterday, he'd told Carrie he'd bought a satellite phone and he'd given her the number. To Carrie the phone meant he might be staying in Alaska longer than he'd originally planned.

The teenagers had been great company yesterday after Brian left. Carrie could tell Lisa was enjoying Ariel's friendship and suspected how isolated the teenager had felt the past few weeks. It was easy to see that the outing was good for Ariel, too. Clearing her idea with the women's shelter, Carrie had asked Ariel if she'd like to stay until Sunday. Ariel had promised to keep an eye on Lisa while she went to Windsor. Carrie assured them she'd call in to see how they were doing. She gave them both her cell phone number and left Brian's numbers on the refrigerator.

Ever since her conversation with Brian after his mother called, Carrie had felt the need to see her own mother, talk to her, lay the past to rest for good.

Before she left, Carrie called her mom to tell her she was on her way and warned both Lisa and Ariel that if they saw even the first signs of labor for Lisa—an achy back, a cramp in her side, a drawing in her womb—they should call Carrie. She could be back in ninety minutes. There was one of Verna's casseroles in the refrigerator thawing for supper in case she was later than she planned.

Rain poured down as Carrie drove, and she thought about Brian and Alaska and the type of weather he might be having. The nights would be long there now.

When Carrie reached the Bradleys' house, her mother opened the door. The ranch-style home covered with white siding and trimmed with blue shutters was compact and perfect for her parents.

Her mother said, "You should have come through the garage so you wouldn't get wet."

Carrie dropped her hood back on her shoulders and smiled. "I won't melt."

As her mom held the door wide, Carrie could already smell baked goods. "I hope you didn't go to a lot of trouble."

"Not a lot. I made that lemon pudding cake. Come on in. I called Whitney and Mary. They'll be here in about an hour."

Carrie's father sat in the recliner she and Brian had bought him for Christmas. He gave her a big smile when he saw her. "Hi, baby."

Carrie went over to her father and hunkered down beside his chair. "How are you doing, Dad?"

He studied her for a few moments. "Not so bad. Did your mom tell you I've been going to that indoor pool the school built? It's open to the public a couple evenings a week. It seems to make my back and leg feel better."

"Dad, I've told you all along if you want to go to therapy, or if a hot tub would make things better—"

"Carrie, darlin', you've paid for enough. And I don't want to drain insurance we might need later. I had enough therapy after the accident to last me a lifetime. And a hot tub? Well, I can't get no exercise in that. But I can in the pool. Hank's been driving me."

Hank Conroy, one of the men her dad had worked with a long time back, was one of his few friends who'd stayed in touch.

"Hank's getting a potbelly," her dad explained. "He wants to try and do something about that."

Carrie studied her dad's weathered face, his brown hair with its receding hairline, his eyes which ever since his injury had held pain. Today, there seemed to be something else there, too. "I'm glad you're getting out." Carrie patted his hand. "When your TV show is over, you come tell me all about it."

After Paula took Carrie's coat, she carried it to the laundry room to let it dry. Carrie wandered into the kitchen, where the lemon cake was sitting on the counter.

Her mother came in saying, "I made chicken salad for lunch."

"That sounds great."

"Want a cup of tea?"

Carrie could see that her mom had already set a few

packs of different types of herbal teas on the table. The teakettle was just beginning to steam. "A cup of tea would be good. I'm going to give Lisa a call to make sure everything's okay."

A few minutes later Carrie had learned the girls were giving each other pedicures. She told her mother that.

Paula smiled. "You like having this girl around, don't you?"

"It's like taking care of Brenda, Whitney and Mary all over again. Yes, I like having her there."

Her mother tore open a package of cranberry tea then dunked the tea bag into her cup of hot water. "I'm glad Whitney and Mary won't be here for a little while."

"Why?"

Her mother hesitated, dipped her tea bag a few more times and wiped her fingers on her napkin. "I told your father."

Carrie wasn't sure what her mother meant. "You told him what?"

"I told him about your rape and abortion and why it's so hard for you to have kids."

Carrie felt as if the floor had dropped from beneath her. "Why? Why did you tell him now after all this time? I don't know if I'm going to be able to look at him now. He must think—"

Suddenly she heard her dad's unsteady gait behind her. He was in the kitchen, too, leaning against the counter. "I don't think anything different about you, Carrie, than I ever did. I knew something awful had happened to you. You didn't eat, you didn't sleep, you didn't come out of your room. Your mother said you had the flu and you were exhausted. I'm not that stupid."

"I never thought you were stupid, George," Paula said.

"You must have thought I wouldn't care. You must have thought I was so lost in myself that what happened to Carrie didn't matter. I guess I was or I would have pushed for explanations. Maybe I just didn't want to know. Maybe I couldn't bear the thought of something happening to one of my little girls."

"Oh, Daddy," Carrie whispered, tears coming to her eyes.

Her father had never been openly affectionate and now he stood where he was, leaning on the counter for support, as straight and rigid as his body could get. "I guess it makes me feel a little better that you never told your sisters, either. Just your mama and your agent."

"I couldn't tell anyone. I felt so ashamed…so worthless. Then time passed and I didn't want to talk about it. I wanted to forget it."

"Have you forgotten it?"

"No."

After he appraised her steadily, her father sighed. "You should tell Brian."

Her answer was automatic. "I can't. I'm afraid he'll leave."

Her father's voice held more strength than she'd ever heard from him. "If you tell him and he leaves, then you shouldn't be together."

"I love him, Dad. I can't bear the thought—" Her voice broke.

Her father crossed to her and put his hand on her shoulder. "Of a life without Brian? I get that. I don't know what I would have done all these years without your mother. But I gotta ask you, Carrie, what kind of marriage do you have if you can't tell him the truth?"

Carrie looked into her dad's brown eyes. The life he

had been through had taught him things she'd never know. But she believed if she ever told Brian the truth, she'd have to be strong enough to accept his leaving.

Standing, she gave her father a hug and felt his arms go around her. "I'll think about it, Dad."

But there seemed to be so much at stake right now, she didn't know if she'd ever find the courage to let her husband go.

Ten

Dusk was settling over Windsor as Carrie said good-bye to her parents, Whitney, Mary, their husbands and children. She went to her car and started the ignition, then backed out of the driveway. Her mother came outside and waved as Carrie drove down the street. After Carrie honked her horn, she concentrated on the drive back to Portland. It had been an odd day, and the repercussions of it were still rattling around inside of her.

After all these years, Carrie had never expected her mother to tell her father exactly what had happened when Carrie was eighteen. But she had.

Before Whitney and Mary had arrived, Carrie had asked her mother, "Why now?"

Paula had responded, "Because it's a barrier between your dad and me. Because life is too short, and I'm getting too old to watch my words. But most of all, because

I needed to admit what I had done. I had to get rid of that weight. Not that I ever will. But sharing it with him has helped. Back then I didn't think he was strong enough to deal with it all. But about six months ago, he sent for a carving kit. He started spending a lot of time in the basement. He's been carving decoys. And Hank even sold a few for him at the senior center. I think he's gotten his self-respect back. Not only that, but for Christmas this year, he carved an elk for me and gave me a card that said he still remembered the one we saw on our honeymoon when we went to Alaska. I guess it made me realize that no matter what happens, we have each other. We'll always have each other."

Carrie's mom had showed her the elk then, and it was beautiful—as beautiful as the acceptance in her father's eyes after she'd hugged him. Maybe his pain had helped him understand hers.

As Carrie drove, she considered her father's advice to tell Brian. Yet even as she considered it, phrases Brian had used just in the past few weeks came back to haunt her. *Fear doesn't absolve her. I expect the truth. A choice I can't forgive.*

Between thoughts of Brian and her parents, Carrie thought about her enjoyment of playing with her nieces and nephews. When she considered the idea of becoming a mother, it filled her with anticipation and excitement, and she could almost push everything else away. All of it was like a merry-go-round in her head as she drove, as the rain pelted the hood of her car and water sluiced across the highway.

About a half hour from Portland, she thought about calling Lisa, but driving on the wet, puddled road required all of her concentration. She'd have to drive Ariel back to the shelter tonight. She hated to do that. But maybe she could help her find a job—

One moment Carrie was watching the taillights on the car in front of her, the next that car listed to the left and fishtailed right. With only an instant to react, she steered her car to the left and went off the shoulder of the road into the guardrail. Although her seat belt held her, the angle of the impact pulled her sideways and her head banged into the door frame.

All light left her world. She was catapulted into a black quagmire where everything was silent.

The cabin in Deep Gulch, Alaska, was heated by a woodstove and had few amenities. There was a cot with a narrow, thin mattress and wool blankets. Brian had melted snow for drinking and a bit of cooking. The scarred old table was accompanied by two rickety wood chairs. It had suited Brian as he'd studied topographical maps by the light of a kerosene lamp. Often his thoughts veered toward Carrie after the day of flying over locations. He'd come back to the cabin hungry and tired.

However, suddenly as he'd sat down to work, he'd lost his appetite and his heart had begun racing. It was an odd sensation, almost like a blow.

Going to the cabin door, he'd taken in lungfuls of cold air and stared out over the white barren landscape. In the silence, he'd experienced a twisting yearning in his gut for Carrie that he couldn't understand. It had been so strong that he'd used the satellite phone to call her. She hadn't answered at the house, nor had Lisa. Carrie hadn't answered on her cell phone, either. That was unlike her.

After an hour, the panicked sensation quieted to a whisper of concern that hadn't left him as he'd worked.

Leaning away from the lantern and the map in his creaky chair, he studied the notes he'd made over the past two days.

However, when a series of beeps emanated from the SAT phone on the cot, he almost turned over the chair in his hurry to reach it. He told himself it could be Ted, it could be Derrick, it could be the pilot.

But none of those voices met his ear. "Mr. Summers?" Lisa asked in a shaky voice.

"Yes. Lisa, is that you?"

"I've been trying to reach you for the last hour. The call wouldn't go through."

"Sometimes there's interference on these phones. What's wrong?"

"It's Carrie. She's been in an accident!"

His heart stopped. "Is she all right?"

"She's hurt. There were four cars involved. Her airbag didn't pop because the *side* of her car hit the guardrail."

He swore. "How badly was she injured?"

"They're running tests. She's still unconscious." Her voice broke. "Can you come home?"

"The pilot dropped me here, then went to make a delivery in another village."

"You've got to come back here, Mr. Summers. Carrie needs you. We don't know what to do."

Carrie had been right about this trip. He never should have left Portland. Not only was he worried sick about her and chomping at the bit to get to her, but all this stress wasn't good for Lisa and her baby, either. "Lisa, I want to talk to her doctor. Can you give him my number?"

"She doesn't have just one doctor. What if he can't get through to you like I couldn't get through?"

"He will if he keeps trying. If he doesn't get through to me, I just need a name so I can have him paged."

"I'll ask one of the nurses at the desk, but I—"

The teenager's voice was trembling. He could hear the tears that threatened to spill over. "Lisa, I want you to take a cab and go back to the house. You need to rest and calm down."

"How am I going to calm down when I don't know how Carrie is? If she's going to wake up? Ariel's here with me. We're going to wait in the lounge."

Brian knew how stubborn Lisa could be. "All right. But you have to promise me something."

"What?"

"After you've talked to the nurse, I want you to rest on the sofa and put your feet up. Have Ariel bring you a glass of milk from the cafeteria."

Silence met his suggestion.

"Lisa?"

"You don't want anything to happen to the baby," she said, as if she understood.

"I don't want anything to happen to *you*. Now please, get me the doctor's name. After you do that, I'm going to call the pilot and see if he can fly me out of here tonight. I'll be back there as soon as I can."

A few minutes later when Brian clicked off the phone, he felt as if he'd lost touch with the rest of the world. Where had Carrie gone today? And what had caused the accident? He realized he was thinking about those questions because he couldn't think about his wife asleep…maybe never waking up.

By the time the doctor returned Brian's call, Brian had almost worn a path on the wood floor in the small cabin. But the pilot couldn't get him out until morning and there was nothing he could do about that. He felt powerless. The feeling made him want to punch his fist through the cabin wall.

When Carrie's doctor spoke to him, worry receded somewhat. Carrie was awake now. She had a concussion and her shoulder had taken most of the impact from hitting the door and was bruised. Her doctor intended to watch her closely over the next twelve hours, and he kept insisting she was one very lucky woman.

Brian decided he was one very lucky man.

The wait for morning seemed interminable. Although he left Deep Gulch early, everything about the return trip seemed to be in slow motion.

Finally, he was there in her hospital room and Lisa was glaring at him reproachfully. "Where have you been?" she asked under her breath, as she met him at the door.

"A weather front moved in last night and I couldn't get out until this morning. Why? Has something changed?"

Lisa's face was pale and drawn, and she looked exhausted. "No. She called for you in the middle of the night and you weren't here."

"Did you stay with her all night?"

"Yes, I stayed with her all night. She didn't have anybody else here. She didn't want me to call her parents, didn't want to worry them."

Guilt stabbed deep, but Brian's defenses slipped into place. "Well, I'm here now. Did you say your friend was with you?" Brian glanced around.

"She's in the lounge. She stuck with me all night."

Brian grabbed a few bills from his wallet. "You and Ariel get something to eat before you leave. Then call a cab to take you back home. Rest. I think the doctor's going to discharge Carrie later today. I'll call you and let you know what's happening."

Brian looked over Lisa's shoulder again. Carrie still seemed to be sleeping.

"You won't forget to call me?"

"I promise I won't forget." As Lisa began to leave the room, Brian laid his hand on her shoulder. "Thank you, Lisa."

She looked surprised at his thanks, then she conjured up a smile and headed for the lounge.

Brian approached Carrie's bed slowly, as if she were Sleeping Beauty. She looked pale. The faded hospital gown and a crisp white pillowcase under her head didn't help.

Dragging the chair beside the bed, he sank into it, and took one of her hands between his.

Her eyes fluttered open. He would have kissed her then, but her words stopped him. "What are you doing here?"

"Lisa called me. Didn't she tell you?"

Carrie shook her head and then winced. The movement must have made her head hurt. Suddenly, Brian knew why Lisa hadn't told Carrie she'd called him. The teenager hadn't been sure he'd come home. Didn't she realize how much he cared about Carrie?

His wife's eyes were troubled now as she murmured, "You had to cut your trip short. Brian, I'm sorry. I'm fine, really. You shouldn't have done that."

Didn't she want him here? Was she was afraid he was going to be angry because he couldn't finish what he'd started in Alaska? Was she concerned now he'd have to go back?

Studying her closely, he knew he couldn't read her any more. That worried him almost as much as her accident. "I've accomplished most of what I set out to do. I just had to cancel today's meetings. Ted will be flying to Anchorage to meet with investors."

"This deal is so important to you."

"*You're* important, too, Carrie."

As she appeared to absorb his words, she still didn't smile. She seemed so far away, even though he was holding her hand, even though he could lean forward a couple of feet and kiss her. "Tell me what happened yesterday. Where had you gone?"

"I went home."

For a moment he was blank. Then he realized she meant somewhere other than their house. "To your mother's?"

"Yes. I hadn't seen them since Christmas, and—" She hesitated and then quickly added, "Whitney and Mary came over. It was just for a couple of hours. Ariel stayed with Lisa. Are they still here?"

"I sent them to get something to eat and gave them cab money home. To our house."

"Lisa's been here since Nancy Allen called her."

"Nancy was in the emergency room when you came in?"

"Yes. She didn't know where to get hold of you, and when she called the house, Lisa answered. Lisa was here every time I woke up."

There was definitely a bond between Carrie and Lisa, a bond he was beginning to feel, too. "Lisa said you didn't want her to call your parents. Do you want me to call them now?"

"No. I'm fine, Brian, really." Carrie began to sit up, but her breath caught and her hand went to her head.

"You're not fine."

"The doctor's releasing me this afternoon."

"Maybe so. But that doesn't mean you can go back to your normal activities. I'm going to find your doctor and see what's going on."

Brian was still holding her hand, but now she pulled it away from him, nervously, it seemed to him, and brushed her hair behind her ear. "I must look a mess. I had no idea you'd come back this soon."

His gut twisted at her words. He realized not only didn't she trust him, but she didn't depend on him. That cut deep because he'd felt he'd never been anything *but* dependable. Sure, he'd worked hard. But usually she could reach him with a phone call. Usually he could put aside what he was doing for an emergency. Gazing into her eyes right now, he felt as if they were almost strangers.

Pushing himself to his feet, he said gruffly, "I'll find out when you're going to be discharged." Then he left his wife's room, worried about her and just as worried about their marriage.

A few hours later, Brian took Carrie home. She kept insisting she was fine, but he knew she wasn't. The prescriptions he'd had filled for her proved she wasn't. In addition, she was supposed to ice her shoulder for the next forty-eight hours. He'd wanted to carry her up to their bedroom, but the expression on her face told him she wouldn't allow that. Before she'd agree to go upstairs to rest, she'd made certain Lisa was fine.

Ariel was still with her and she said to Carrie, "I'm glad to see you're okay, Mrs. Summers. Now that you're home, I'll go back to the shelter."

"I want to talk to you before you leave," Brian said.

Ariel looked puzzled. "What about?"

"Finding you a job so you can get back on your feet. How do you feel about filing and general office work to start?"

"Anything would be great. As soon as I can save enough for a security deposit, I can get my own place again."

"I might be able to find you a place that doesn't require a security deposit. I have to do some checking. We'll talk about it before you leave." He turned to Carrie. "Come on. Let's get you up to bed."

However, before Brian shepherded her away, she said to Ariel, "Thanks for sticking by Lisa."

"We're friends," Ariel said. "It was no big deal."

"Friendship is always a big deal," Carrie murmured with a wan smile for both girls.

Carrie took the steps slowly because every bone in her body hurt. The doctor had ordered a CT scan, but said everything looked normal. He'd also taken X rays of her shoulder. She *had* been fortunate.

Once in the bedroom, Carrie slipped into the bathroom and when she emerged she was wearing a pale blue nightshirt.

Brian had turned back the covers for her. "Is there anything you'd like? Something to drink? Something to eat? You barely picked at lunch."

"I'm not hungry." She slid into bed and covered herself with the sheet. "Are you really going to give Ariel a job?"

"Yes. One of the clerks left and I was going to call the temp agency. Instead, I'll give Ariel a chance. We'll see how she does. If she's competent, she'll be doing a lot more than filing before long."

There were a few moments of silence. "Thank you, Brian."

"For what?"

"For giving Ariel this job so she can get out of the shelter. For sending Lisa back home to rest this morning after you got there. For coming home."

Something about Carrie's attitude bothered him. He wondered if she was still upset about their argument after they'd made love in the hot tub. Or was there something else? She was avoiding his gaze. She was putting distance between them. On top of that, she was much too pale.

What he wanted to do was climb into bed beside her and take her into his arms. But for some reason, his instincts told him she wouldn't allow that right now. Maybe she was just trying to get her bearings after what had happened to her. The police had taken a statement from her this afternoon before she'd left the hospital. Brian had learned the car in front of her had blown a tire and everything else had stemmed from that.

He sat on the bed beside her. "I'm going to send Ariel back in a cab. I'd take her myself, but I'm afraid Lisa will run up and down the steps to see how you are if I leave. As far along as she is, she shouldn't be doing that."

"I don't want her worrying about me."

"I'll try to reassure her."

Carrie put her hand to her forehead and Brian asked, "Is your headache worse?"

"The doctor said it should go away in a day or two."

Brian couldn't help but touch Carrie then. He couldn't keep from reaching out and stroking her cheek. "Lisa's call took ten years off my life. When she said you were in an accident and were still unconscious…"

"I'm sorry I worried you. I shouldn't have been so close to the car in front of me, but I was thinking and—" She looked away from him.

"Thinking about what?"

Her words came slowly. "My family. You. Lisa. A baby."

Tears welled up in her eyes, and Brian wished he could crawl inside her head and see what she was really thinking. He wiped away one of her tears with his thumb. "You rest. Do you want me to sit here with you?"

She shook her head. "That's not necessary. I know you have things to do."

Though almost angry that she didn't think she was just as important as any of those things, he realized he should be angry at himself, not at her, if he'd always given her the impression that work had to come first. "I'm going to talk to Ariel for a bit and then work in my office. If you need anything, call on the intercom. Even if I don't hear from you, I'll be up in about a half an hour. I won't wake you if you're sleeping." Leaning forward, he pressed a soft kiss onto her forehead.

She closed her eyes.

As he stood, she didn't open her eyes again or say anything. When he left the room, he felt as if he had a lead weight in his chest.

Something was very wrong. He had an idea that might make it better. After Ariel left, he'd surf real estate sites on the Internet and find exactly what he was looking for.

Although Carrie adhered to her doctor's orders to rest for twenty-four hours, she chafed at the idea of it. Yes, she had a headache and her shoulder was sore when she moved it. But she could function. She didn't want to be stuck in her room upstairs. However, Brian had insisted, along with her doctor. Brian even stayed home from work all day Monday, checking on her every now and then.

She had too much time to think.

By Tuesday morning, she'd decided she'd had enough of resting. She wanted to spend some time with Lisa.

She had withdrawn from Brian since the accident, since her visit to her parents. That was because she couldn't look him in the eye without wanting to spill everything to him. But there was so much at stake. Not only their marriage, but the future of Lisa's baby. Brian *was* changing—cutting back his hours, cutting back on the traveling. Maybe her life would right itself again, and she'd never have to tell him what she'd done.

On Tuesday afternoon, Carrie realized her headache was almost gone. While she'd spent the morning with Lisa, Verna had been cooking in the kitchen. After she and Lisa ate clam chowder and sandwiches for lunch, Carrie asked Verna to make chocolate mousse for dessert that night since it was Lisa's favorite.

"Do you mind if I have a friend over tomorrow night?" Lisa asked Carrie before dinner.

As Carrie set the table she asked, "Ariel?"

"No. It's a guy. Craig Latimore. He worked at the deli where Ariel and I hung out. He used to give us handouts when no one was looking."

"That was kind of him."

Lisa blushed a little. "Yeah, I guess. Anyway, when Ariel and I got breakfast at the hospital the other morning, he was in the cafeteria, too. His aunt was having gallbladder surgery. I used to think he felt sorry for me and Ariel. But when I told him I was giving the baby up for adoption, he asked if he could see me sometime."

Carrie's motherly instincts went on alert. "How old is he?"

"He's twenty."

Going still, Carrie studied Lisa. "Do you like him?"

"He looked out for me and Ariel. He came and checked on us when we were sleeping in a vacant building before we went to the shelter. Craig's the one who convinced us we'd be better off there."

From everything Lisa said it sounded as if this Craig cared about her. But Carrie would like to see for herself. One of the best ways to do that was to have him over to the house. "Sure, he can come over tomorrow evening."

"Do you mind if we just order pizza or something? We don't have to bother you and Mr. Summers."

"I don't know what Brian's doing tomorrow night."

"He might not like Craig."

"Why not?"

"Because Craig rides a motorcycle. And he has tattoos and earrings. He got his eyebrow pierced a few months ago, too. Maybe you should warn Mr. Summers."

"Maybe *you* should warn him," Carrie encouraged with a smile.

Lisa shrugged. "We'll see. Mr. Summers might not even be home. No use getting him all riled over nothing."

Avoidance. She was practicing it herself these days. She couldn't blame Lisa for wanting to take the easy way out.

When Brian called to tell Carrie he wouldn't be home for supper, she didn't think anything of it. After all, he'd taken off all day yesterday.

But after she said good-night to Lisa and sat in her bedroom, fatigue caught up with her. She was reclining on the sofa, listening to music in their sitting area, when Brian came in with a wide smile and an envelope in his hand. He'd already taken off his suit jacket and unknotted his tie.

Now he tossed both on the chair beside the bed and crossed to her. "How do you feel?"

"Much better than yesterday."

Lowering himself beside her, he studied her. "But you overdid it today, didn't you?"

"I didn't do much. I mostly kept Lisa company."

"Your body needs to recover from what you've been through. You've got to give it time."

Pushing herself into a sitting position, she promised, "I'll give it time. But I can't stay up here in bed. The headache's gone, and as long as I don't lift anything, I'm fine."

"I'm convinced," he said with a laugh, though she could see he wasn't. He wasn't going to press her, but he was still going to watch over her.

"I have something to show you." Lowering himself beside her on the sofa, he unfastened the clip on the envelope and pulled out two pages of photographs. "I took these today, and I'd like you to look at them."

She took the two glossy sheets of digital photos and studied them. On one page the pictures were all scenery—pines and alders and maples. In one photograph she could make out a narrow stream. "This looks like a beautiful property."

"It is. Look at the other one."

On the other sheet the setting was wooded, too. But in the midst of it sat a one-story house, all cedar and glass. Photographs captured the house from different angles. A wide shot showed split-rail fence surrounding the property.

"That looks lovely, too." She turned curious eyes to Brian's.

"I know you've always thought this house was too big. When we got married, I thought it was the kind of place you'd want, and that's why I went ahead with the deal. But you like Leigh and Adam's home, so…"

He pointed to the pictures of scenery first. "We could build exactly what you want right here. It's a beautiful property. I know the developer. If you want a log home like Adam and Leigh have, or something more traditional, we could plan it together." Then he ran his thumb over the other sheet of photographs. "On the other hand, this one's already built. It's only about a quarter of a mile from Leigh and Adam. It's about five years old. The man who built it is changing jobs and moving to Seattle. I walked through it today, and it's quality. It's one floor, four bedrooms, which would be great because I could use one for my office. Other than that, it's pretty compact, with a kitchen, dining room and family room. I think you'd like it."

Carrie was totally stunned by what her husband was proposing. "But you like this house."

"I did. But it *is* big. And after being in Adam's house, I understand what you mean by not feeling lived-in. You can't shout from one room to the other here. Our baby will be crawling around and get lost!"

Brian's expression said he actually cared about that, and Carrie felt tears come to her eyes. Brian *was* changing. He'd listened to what she'd said and was trying to do something about it. "I would love a smaller, cozier house. But only if that's what *you* want, too."

"What I want is for you to go along and look at it with me as soon as you're feeling better. It hasn't been listed yet, and the owner's going to give us first look. I don't want you to feel pressured, either. If not this one, we'll find something else. Or we'll build."

Feeling lighter than she had in weeks, Carrie kissed his cheek. "Looking at a house won't be too strenuous. Let's go tomorrow."

"You're sure?"

"I'm positive."

"All right. I'll come home around three. If for some reason you don't feel like it, just let me know. We have time, Carrie."

Did they have time? Right now she felt closer to Brian than she had in weeks. Was that because they now had a common goal? A home with a child in it. Isn't that what they'd always wanted?

Brian pushed the pictures back into the envelope. Then he surrounded Carrie with his arm and leaned back against the sofa. "I haven't had supper yet, so I'm going to go down and see what leftovers are in the refrigerator. Would you like a cup of tea?"

"You don't have to—"

Leaning close he kissed her temple. "I want to. Then we'll just snuggle up and watch the news together."

He was telling her he wouldn't make love with her until she was ready, until she felt her body was ready. How long had it been since they'd just lain together holding each other?

"I'd like that," she murmured, her voice catching.

Brian gave her a squeeze and rested his jaw on top of her head. "Everything's going to be all right, Carrie. You'll see."

Carrie desperately wanted to believe Brian's words. She would believe them. That was all there was to it.

Eleven

When Carrie and Brian returned from their outing to visit the wooded property and the house the following day, Carrie felt as if she'd just found the pot of gold at the end of the rainbow. She'd liked the house a lot and Brian had seemed as enthusiastic about it as she was. They'd spent time in it, poking into cupboards, turning faucets off and on, admiring the wood trim.

Afterward Brian had taken her by the shoulders and asked, "Are you sure you don't want to build? We could custom design everything."

"I'd custom design it just like this," she'd told him, loving the blue-and-green motifs in the kitchen, the beautiful ceramic tile floors in the bathrooms. "What I like best of all is that we're right down the road from Leigh and Adam."

"Should I call the owner with a figure?"

Slow, thick, honeylike happiness had flowed through Carrie then. She'd nodded, and Brian had kissed her—a long, sweet kiss that had made her dizzy.

As Brian followed Carrie into the kitchen now, she said, "Lisa was going to have a friend over. But I didn't see his—"

"His what?" Brian asked Carrie curiously.

"His motorcycle. He rides one. And, from what I understand, he had his eyebrow pierced, too."

A look of consternation came into Brian's eyes, but he didn't express it, possibly because he didn't want to break the mood between them.

"Maybe it's just as well he didn't show up," Brian murmured with a wry smile.

However, when they went to the family room, they heard voices and found Lisa and the boy sharing pizza, laughing and watching a video on TV. The laughter stopped at once as Brian and Carrie entered the room.

Lisa introduced Craig, watching Brian all the while.

Afterward Brian said, "Carrie tells me you have a motorcycle."

"I parked it in the back. I didn't want anybody stealing it if it was out front."

"We rarely have theft in this neighborhood, but I guess it's always a possibility."

Carrie could see Brian was trying to give the boy the benefit of the doubt, one he hadn't given Lisa at first look. Craig's brown hair was long on one side and stood up on the other. His T-shirt proclaimed, "Ron's Deli Rocks." His jeans were tattered, but Carrie suspected he might have bought them that way. Despite the oversized jeans and T-shirt, she could tell he was slim and tall.

When an awkward silence settled over the room,

Lisa motioned to the half pizza on the coffee table. "Do you want some?" Her eyes danced with teasing sparkles, and Carrie knew full well she didn't expect Brian to accept.

But to both Lisa's and Carrie's surprise he replied, "Sure. We could order another one so we're sure we have plenty. What movie are you watching?"

"It's a chick flick," muttered Craig.

The outing had tired Carrie out and she realized she still wasn't back to normal. As she and Brian joined the teenagers, she merely nibbled on her slice of pizza. She just wasn't hungry.

After Brian questioned Craig about his hobby of working on motorcycles, he looked over at Carrie's un-eaten slice of pizza. His two were finished.

Standing, he held out his hand to her. "Come on. Let's go upstairs and look at those pictures I took on the digital camera. If you kids need anything—"

"We'll be fine, Mr. Summers," Lisa assured him.

Brian gave Lisa a look that said he didn't know if he should leave her alone with this young man, but he did.

At the foot of the stairs, he studied Carrie. "You're pale. I kept you too long at the house, didn't I?"

"No, you didn't. I had a wonderful time looking at it with you. But my shoulder is hurting, and I'm feeling a little queasy. Sometimes the medicine does that."

"Then why don't you go upstairs and crawl into bed? I'll print out the pictures we took and bring them up."

When he started for his office, she clasped his elbow. "Brian."

"What?"

"Thank you."

"For what?"

"For finding the house. For understanding how I feel about it."

"I feel the same way," he admitted. "Now go on. Get comfortable. Before I come up, I'll make sure Craig isn't dismantling his motorcycle in our family room."

Smiling, Carrie climbed the stairs. Whether Brian realized it or not, he was acting like a father. No matter how his relationship with Lisa had begun, now they were developing ties, and Carrie loved seeing that.

Nevertheless, as she undressed she felt more and more exhausted. After she hung her clothes in the closet, she slid a nightgown over her head, crawled into bed and turned on the TV. Within minutes she couldn't keep her eyes open.

At first sleep was comforting, warm, enveloping her in a soft blanket that seemed to float with visions of pine trees and split-rail fence. A large picture window flitted through her dreams with happy feelings and a sense of hope.

However the blue and green and golden pictures diminished and eventually faded away. Although she was still wrapped in the blanket, she felt lost. A twisting of anxiety began in her womb and worked itself up through her chest.

Darker pictures now swam around her—a city street at midnight. The smell of wet asphalt steamed by summer heat assaulted her senses. She didn't know what was coming, but she knew it wasn't going to be good. She tried to shout "No!" and maybe even did. Struggling against the blanket, she strove to break free. But it imprisoned her.

Suddenly there was a man standing in front of her. He was wearing ugly green scrubs and he held a large scalpel. But his face... At first it was a doctor's face, the doctor who had taken her baby away. Then the face changed. Instead of brown hair and a weak jaw and pale-blue eyes, the man was wearing a black ski mask. She knew what that meant. She knew who he was. He was wielding the scalpel, coming toward her.

She couldn't escape the blanket. Thrashing about, she punched it, scraped at it with her nails and yelled "No" so loud her head ached.

"Carrie! Carrie!" A deep, strong voice called.

When she felt an arm imprison her, she fought it, twisted, turned—

A low oath cut through her unconsciousness. Her shoulder hurt as she battered against the restraint.

"Carrie. It's Brian. Wake up!"

That determined voice. *Wake up*. Brian. It was Brian.

When her eyes fluttered open, Brian's face was close to hers and he was holding her tight.

"Wake up, Carrie. You're going to hurt yourself."

Hurt herself. Hurt him. Hurt them both.

Conscious of her surroundings, she saw Brian and she stilled. Her breaths were coming in hard, sharp gasps. Her hair was matted around her face and sweat beaded on her forehead. She was shaking, and her hands were as clammy as they'd been that night....

At first she was still hazy and almost pushed Brian away, confusing him with the men who had hurt her. But then she realized who he was, who *she* was, where they were. The smothering fog that had wrapped her in its grip broke, and she took more deep, calming breaths.

"What's wrong? Are you okay? It's me. Look at me."

She couldn't meet Brian's eyes. She just couldn't. She covered her face with her hands, felt the lump of tears in her throat, but knew she couldn't cry. If she told Brian about everything, he'd hate her. She just knew it. They were starting to find their way again, and she didn't want to lose everything she held dear.

Although she wouldn't look at her husband, his arm went around her. His warm body comforted her as a silence stretched between them like a long road they couldn't travel.

Finally he asked softly, "What was that all about?"

Finding her voice, she managed, "It was a nightmare. Just a nightmare. I think I'm worried about Lisa and her baby. Our baby."

"Afraid she won't give him up for adoption?"

"I guess. I don't know. You know how nightmares are. Sort of symbolic. Everything all mixed up together."

"The last time you had a nightmare it was after the surgery to try to unblock your tubes. Was it the same one?"

Brian had remembered. That one had been similar, but not quite as terrifying. "I wasn't concerned about Lisa and the baby then."

"No, you weren't. But I imagine there's some common denominator."

She shook her head, and her hair brushed against his bare shoulder. "You can't explain dreams, Brian. They're a slice of life thrown at you all at once. They usually don't make sense."

"This wasn't a dream, Carrie. It was a nightmare. Something bad was happening in it. Don't you want to talk about it?"

There it was—the opening. Her chance to lay everything at his feet. She'd be totally naked and vulnerable before him.

Right now, when she was still trembling from the vividness of the nightmare, she couldn't imagine doing that. "I don't want to relive it," she murmured.

This time Brian didn't give her the choice of looking at him. With his index finger, he nudged her face around to meet his gaze. Studying her, he must have seen the remnants of terror. He must have seen the raw emotion still swirling inside of her. He must have seen how very tired she was.

Reaching to his side of the bed, he switched off the light. Then he slid down and stretched his arm out to her. "Come here. If I hold you, nothing bad will happen to you."

Curling into his body, she laid her head in the crook of his shoulder. She did feel protected by him, but she also had something to fear from him. Rejection.

For now she'd concentrate on the comfort and try to get some sleep. In the morning she'd deal with the rest.

Brian was up before Carrie the next morning. He showered and dressed and watched her as she slept. There was something going on with her, and he wanted to know what it was. Yet he couldn't bully it out of her. She had to trust him enough to tell him, whether it was her concerns about adopting Lisa's baby, some problem with her family or maybe a desire to go back to work. Whatever it was, it was reinforcing a barrier between them.

Her accident had made her seem more vulnerable, and he supposed that was only natural. However, even in that vulnerability, she was fighting against him caring for her, doing things for her.

Was she resentful because he hadn't welcomed Lisa with open arms? Was she still concerned because at the beginning he hadn't embraced adoption wholeheartedly?

Only Carrie had the answers.

Whatever was bothering her was stressing her out, as was evident in that nightmare last night. Maybe she was having post-traumatic stress from the accident. Another checkup with her doctor might be in order.

When Brian went downstairs to the kitchen he found Lisa pouring herself a glass of orange juice. "I heard Craig leave about eleven," he said.

"That wasn't after my curfew, was it?" Lisa gave him a sly smile.

"No. At eighteen, curfews should be a thing of the past."

"Sometimes I feel that you treat me like a kid. But then other times you treat me like an adult."

"That's probably because we're watching over you. That makes me feel as if I have a stake in what you do."

After she drank some of the juice, she asked, "Do you think I'll hear from the colleges soon?"

"Probably in a few weeks. I read your essays. They were good—especially the one that explained how being homeless feels." He'd been pleased to see Lisa wasn't only a good writer, but she could express herself so facilely.

When Lisa didn't respond, he went over to the cupboard and took out a frying pan. "I was going to make Carrie some breakfast. Do you want to help?"

"Sure. She's made stuff for me plenty of times. I can scramble eggs."

"That sounds good. I'll fry the bacon and toast the bread."

When Lisa crossed the room to the refrigerator, she suddenly doubled over.

Brian was beside her in an instant. "What's wrong?"

"I'm not sure. It was a cramp." As she straightened, she must have felt it again because she twisted away from him and leaned on the counter.

"What's going on?" Carrie's worried voice came from the doorway. She was dressed in a colorful sweater and black leggings, and looked rested, with only a faint hint of blue under her eyes.

"I don't know," Brian replied. "She said she had a cramp."

Lisa gave a little squeal and Carrie was beside her. "I'm going to call your doctor."

"Do you think these are contractions?" Lisa asked.

"It's possible. Babies often come early. Let us help you into the family room, and I'll call her."

Twenty minutes later, Brian was in the doctor's waiting room, and Carrie was accompanying Lisa with the nurse to an examination room. He made a few calls to clear his schedule, not knowing what was going to happen next. Then he alternately worried, paced, tapped his foot and worried some more.

It was an hour later when Lisa and Carrie emerged from the inner offices. Lisa looked upset. "It's not happening now," she said.

Brian waited for an explanation.

Carrie explained, "Pre-labor pains. Sometimes this happens. At least, that's what the doctor said. The baby has dropped and could come any time, but just not right now."

"I'm supposed to go home and wait," Lisa said dejectedly.

Brian could see emotion was close to the surface in both women.

"Let's go home and I'll make you both brunch."

At Carrie's expression he asked, "You don't think I

can scramble a few eggs and fry some slices of bacon? I have hidden talents you know nothing about. I can even flip an egg so the yolk doesn't break."

At that, Carrie smiled, but Lisa still looked distracted.

The teenager was silent the whole way home. Although she sat and watched Brian prepare most of the breakfast as Carrie sliced fruit, she didn't try to enter their conversations.

After eating about half the food on her plate, she laid down her fork and looked at Carrie. "Do you think the doctor was being honest and these contractions are normal in pregnancy?"

"I don't think she would have said it if it wasn't true."

Lisa looked down at her plate. "I'm worried."

"What about?" Brian gently asked.

"When I found out I was pregnant and I came to Portland, I didn't eat right. I didn't take vitamins like the ones advertised in the doctor's office. I didn't have regular checkups. What if…what if something's wrong? What if something happens to me and the baby's born and we haven't signed the papers?"

To his amazement Brian found himself saying, "Carrie and I are committed to adopting this baby, Lisa. We want this child. No matter what, we're going to take him."

"Even if there's something wrong?"

Suddenly, Lisa's attitude worried Brian beyond measure. "You had a sonogram. The doctor has done blood work. There's no indication that anything's wrong. Is there something you're not telling us? Did you take drugs when you were on the streets?"

He heard a small gasp escape Carrie, but he kept his gaze on Lisa.

A loud "No!" exploded from the teenager. "No, I

never took drugs. Never. Well, I mean, a couple of years before I left Seattle I smoked some pot. But I haven't used anything since I came to Portland. Since I've been pregnant. Honest. You've got to believe me."

At one time Brian might not have believed her. But he could hear sincerity in her voice now, and see no deception in her eyes, or defiance, or the rebellion that had emanated from her when she'd first moved in with them. "I believe you."

Carrie reached across the table and took Lisa's hand. "I want you to try to stop worrying."

"I might stop worrying if you and Mr. Summers sign something, so that if something happens to me you'll have the baby. Will you do that? Can you call a lawyer to make it happen?"

As agitated as Lisa was, Brian wanted her to calm down. He also understood her concern. Labor and delivery was a frightening thing to her, and though it didn't happen often now, women *did* die in childbirth.

Glancing at Carrie, he said, "I can phone Trina Bentley or Stacy Williams. They might have a lawyer at Children's Connection who can take care of this."

"Do you want me to do it?" Carrie asked. "I know you intended to go in to work today."

"I've cleared my schedule. This is more important." When he saw his wife's eyes grow moist, he hoped he was seeing tears of happiness because he'd finally realized where his priorities should be.

That night, after Carrie said good-night to Lisa, she went upstairs to the nursery with a hammer and nails and a yardstick. She and Brian had done everything they could today to reassure Lisa that everything was going to be fine. They'd signed documents provided by the lawyer from Children's Connection, and Lisa had gone with them to have the papers notarized. She'd seemed much calmer after that and told Carrie there had been no signs of any further contractions. Now she was watching TV before she turned in for the night.

Carrie glanced around the nursery with a smile, beginning to believe she and Brian would have a baby in their arms soon. She'd already washed the socks and kimonos and playsuits she'd bought, as well as stacked diapers in a holder near the changing table. There were blankets and booties and pacifiers in the drawers, along with infant T-shirts and a tiny snowsuit. All she had to do now was put the finishing touches on the nursery.

She wanted to find a special mobile for the crib. Maybe she could do that tomorrow in the car Brian had rented for her while hers was being repaired. Even if they were going to move, she wanted this room to be a haven for their baby, as pleasant, happy and colorful as it could be. The cream-colored walls were a perfect backdrop for the quilted and padded animals she now hung at intervals around the room—a baby tiger, a baby lamb, a donkey, a kitten, a pup and a seal. She'd also bought framed prints of Huckleberry Finn and Tom Sawyer and hung those, too.

Hearing footsteps in the hall, she swung around and saw Brian. He was carrying a five-foot-tall stuffed giraffe and a few white bags under his arm.

"What's all this?" she asked, smiling.

"I couldn't resist. I bought a teddy bear, too. And one of those things you put in the crib for kids to play with. You know, with the mirrors and the music and the lights."

After he glanced around the room, he set the giraffe by the crib. "This looks nice. I could have helped."

"Pounding in a few nails wasn't very strenuous."

Dropping the bags on the rocking chair, he crossed to her and gently rubbed her shoulder. "How do you feel?"

"Better. Much better."

"Is your shoulder still sore?"

"If I lift something too heavy."

"How about the headaches?"

"I haven't had any today. My hair might turn gray until Lisa has this baby, though. She scared me this morning."

"Scared *you?* I didn't know what to do first, lay her on the floor or call an ambulance."

Carrie laughed. And it felt so good. Being with Brian like this felt so good. She wasn't going to mess it up. She wasn't going to do anything to mar this new life they were planning.

As he looked down at her, Brian's brown eyes became darker, and his expression became more intense. "You know what I'd like to do right now?" he asked huskily.

"What?"

"Carry you into our bedroom and make love to you."

Carrie inhaled Brian's scent. She let her gaze pass over his strong jaw, his straight nose, his high cheekbones, every feature of the man she loved. Sex wasn't the answer to the problems in a marriage. It wasn't the remedy that could take the place of talking. But it was a powerful force, a bond, a tie, a glue.

"I'd like that," she said clearly, so he would know without a doubt that her intentions were the same as his.

When he broke into a broad smile, wonderful sparks lit his eyes. Tonight would be special.

He scooped her up into his arms and carried her to their bed.

Nothing else mattered tonight...absolutely nothing else but her and Brian.

Twelve

Awakening, Carrie sat up in bed.

"Carrie. Carrie!"

Brian was sitting up now, too, as Carrie turned to speak into the intercom. "Lisa? What's wrong?"

"My water broke. The contractions have started again."

"Better get dressed," Brian warned. "This could be it."

Hurrying from the bed, Carrie went to the dresser and pulled out a clean bra and panties. "I hope she doesn't have a long labor. I hope it goes easy for her."

Coming up behind her, Brian encircled her with his arms. "No matter what happens, we're going to be with her. And we're going to be parents, Mrs. Summers."

Before they'd fallen asleep, Brian had made tender love to her. "Yes, we are," she agreed breathlessly as he gave her a tight squeeze and a kiss that told her he was remembering last night as well as looking forward to their future.

A few minutes later they were dressed and rushing down the stairs. When they reached Lisa's room, she was on her bed, looking scared. "We have to change the sheets. We have to..."

By her side, Carrie squeezed her arm. "Don't worry about the sheets. How long between contractions?"

"About five minutes. They started around midnight, but I thought I was just having false labor pains again. I didn't want to call you."

A contraction gripped Lisa, and she took hold of the sheet, squeezing it in her hands. "I don't think I can do this," she cried when it was over.

"Yes, you can. Come on. Let's get you to the hospital," Brian suggested.

"Can you get Lisa's bag?" Carrie asked her husband. "It's right inside the closet. I'll help her into another nightgown and robe. Then we'll go."

Ten minutes later, Brian drove to the hospital while Carrie sat in the back with Lisa and called her doctor.

"She'll meet us there." Carrie clicked off the phone and slipped it into her coat pocket.

"What if the baby wants to come out before Dr. Grieb gets there?" Lisa wailed.

"I'm sure there's a doctor who covers for her. You'll be in good hands, honey. Believe me."

Lisa was crying openly now. "I don't want to do this. Can't they just give me a C-section? Cut me open and take it?"

"They won't do that unless there's a problem. It's best if this all happens naturally. If you have surgery, recuperation will be a lot longer."

"I'm scared," Lisa whispered, her voice trembling.

Putting her arm around the teenager, Carrie drew her close. "I know you are. I'm here with you, and so is Brian."

At the emergency room, Nancy Allen was standing with the wheelchair, waiting. Nancy was a tall woman with short brown hair and sparkling hazel eyes. She had more motherly instincts than anyone Carrie knew. If her romance with Everett worked out, maybe she'd finally have the baby *she'd* always wanted.

As soon as Carrie and Lisa and Brian were within earshot, she explained, "I'm escorting you up to OB. How are you doing, Lisa?"

The teenager just crumpled into the wheelchair.

Nancy patted her shoulder. "Hold on, honey. Pretty soon this will be all over."

As she started wheeling Lisa inside, she looked at Carrie and Brian. "How are you two holding up?"

Brian curved his arm around Carrie's waist as they walked. "We had a scare yesterday. Lisa had false labor pains. But I think this is the real thing. I feel like a soon-to-be father."

"And I can't wait to hold this child in my arms," Carrie added.

The trip upstairs was uneventful. When the nurse in OB came to take charge of Lisa, the teenager looked up at Carrie with beseeching eyes. "Come with me."

The middle-aged nurse smiled encouragingly. "She can get you registered while we prepare you. They'll have to get ready, too."

"Ready?" Lisa looked worried.

"Gowns and hats."

As the nurse wheeled Lisa away, Carrie felt so many

emotions that she wasn't sure what to do with them. Lisa had become like a little sister to her.

"She's so scared," Carrie whispered to Brian.

He gave her a squeeze. "Let's get her registered. Then we can help her through this."

Nancy gave Carrie a quick hug. "I'll check on all of you when I get a break."

The labor went longer than any of them expected, and when Nancy peeked into the birthing room at 7:00 a.m., Carrie knew they all looked exhausted. The doctor was with them now, assuring them Lisa was fully dilated, and soon her baby would be born.

Nancy said, "I'll hang out in the lounge for a little while." She gave Lisa a smile. "You can do this."

The doctor agreed. "Yes, you can. The baby's crowning. Come on, Lisa. I need some really big pushes."

With her hand on Lisa's shoulder, Carrie murmured, "Think about your mom and dad watching over you and giving you all the energy you need."

As another contraction became a wrenching pain inside of her, Lisa moaned.

"Remember how the nurses told you to breathe," Brian reminded her. "Come on. One, two, three, push. One, two, three, push." When he took Lisa's hand in his, Carrie could see he cared about the teenager as much as she did.

Lisa's hair was damp and matted against her head, and her face was ruddy with exertion. Now she pushed with all her might, all her heart, all her determination to get this baby born.

"That's it, Lisa. He's coming. Come on now. One more. Let's get the shoulders out," Dr. Grieb ordered.

With another stupendous burst of energy, Lisa pushed and grunted, and then gave out a loud moan.

"Here he is!"

At the doctor's words two nurses were suddenly at her side, and Carrie wondered if something was wrong.

But then she heard a lusty cry, and the doctor was cutting the cord and placing the baby in Lisa's arms.

Brian held Carrie tight, and he murmured close to her ear, "There's our son."

Tears welled up in her eyes as he kissed her gently. Then they both looked down at the newborn baby, at his brown hair and smooth pink skin.

Lisa was trying to catch her breath, but she looked at her child and ran her thumb down his cheek.

For a moment, Carrie panicked. What if Lisa didn't want to give up the baby now? Then, suddenly, an overwhelming calm overtook her. She and Brian would take them both in. They'd deal with the rest after that.

"Have you thought of a name?" Carrie asked.

Lisa turned to her. "Don't you want to name him? He's beautiful. But I can't be the mother he needs, and you can. He's yours, Carrie."

Leaning down to Lisa, Carrie kissed her forehead. "Thank you. But if you want to name him, that's only fitting."

As Lisa blinked rapidly, tears came to her eyes, and she focused on Brian. "Do you feel the same way?"

"I do. You gave birth to him. You should have the honor."

"All right. I did think about it. I'd like to name him Timothy Jacob—after my dad."

"Timothy Jacob," Brian repeated, as if he were considering the most important matter in the world. "I like it. And I'm sure your father would like it."

The nurse came to take the baby then. "I'm going to get him cleaned up and let you get some rest." Looking from Carrie to Lisa, she explained, "Usually, when a mom gives up a baby for adoption, she doesn't feed him. Is that the case here?"

Again Lisa said to Carrie, "He's yours now."

"I'd love to feed him."

"All right. I'll get his schedule from the doctor and give it to you. It might mean some inconvenient running back and forth, but we can always feed him if you can't get here."

"I'll be here."

"So will I," Brian added in a certain voice.

Carrie was filled with so much love for her husband and their newborn son, she felt as if she'd burst.

Carrie and Brian stayed with Lisa at the hospital until almost noon. Before Carrie left, she went to the nursery to feed her baby. Brian was with her, and as she sat in the rocking chair holding Timothy in her arms, she saw the most tender, amazing expression on Brian's face. He looked as if he'd just been handed the best Christmas gift he'd ever received, and Carrie's throat tightened.

After a nurse showed Carrie an appropriate way to burp the baby, she did that, and then she handed Timothy to her husband. "Do you want to feed him?"

She'd never seen Brian look uncertain, but he did now. "Are you sure that's all right?"

"You're the dad," she replied with a smile, and his answering grin told her again that he was happier at this moment than he'd ever been. Brian finally had the family he'd always wanted, and she'd never do anything to endanger that.

* * *

When Charlie Prescott slipped into the supply closet on the OB/GYN floor after visiting hours that evening, nobody noticed him. As a former janitor at Portland General, he knew every nook and cranny of the place. As a janitor, he'd been faceless. Nobody paid attention to janitors.

On the other hand, Baker was recognizable. And the more Baker had talked, the more Charlie had realized the man could panic or turn tail and run. In this instance he would be a liability. Charlie didn't like liabilities, or taking unnecessary chances. He'd thought about hiring somebody else to steal the Sanders baby. But then he'd have another loose end that had to be tied up. If he did it himself, he could be sure it was done right. He didn't have a couple waiting right now, but he would shortly.

Soon he could take a plane to Brazil and live the good life for the rest of his days—thanks to all the babies he "delivered" to childless couples. He laughed to himself. Charlie "the Stork" Prescott would be retired.

Changing into scrubs, Charlie thought about yesterday when he'd been in here getting the new security code with his telephoto lens. They changed the numbers in the nursery code once a week and thought they had ironclad security. But he was smarter than the suits who ran this place.

Once he was dressed in scrubs, including a hat, he applied makeup that gave him an olive complexion and took tortoiseshell glasses from his pants pocket. Stowing the mirror, makeup and street clothes under a towel on the top shelf of a supply cart, he slipped on latex gloves, draped a sheet over the cart, then made sure the basket on the second shelf was ready for a newborn.

Keycard in hand that he'd pilfered from one of the nurses' lockers, he opened the closet door and pushed the cart around the corner, away from the nursery to a service elevator. There he let it sit. Making sure the elevator door would open as soon as he pressed the button, he took out his cell phone, dialed the hospital's number and asked for the nurses' desk on OB/GYN. When the head nurse answered, he asked for Patty Kirkpatrick. She was the redhead overseeing the babies now.

Moments later, the page came over the loudspeaker system. Patty left the nursery and headed for the desk around the corner.

Charlie made his move.

It was so easy, he almost laughed. After he used the keycard, he punched in the code. Once inside the nursery he easily found the Sanders baby. Picking him up, he wrapped him in another blanket and slipped outside. Within minutes, the baby was inside the basket on the supply cart, and Charlie was in the elevator headed for the basement.

On the ground level, he gathered his clothes, wiped any prints from the supply cart and put the infant in a sling carrier close to his chest, leaving the basket on the cart. Hurrying down a dimly lit corridor, he used the keycard again and punched in another code to let himself outside. Most offices were empty and visitors had left the hospital. The darkness shrouded him as he stayed away from the lighted paths and almost jogged to his car, parked in an annex parking lot. Rain began to fall.

Minutes later, he'd stowed the baby into the infant car seat, climbed in, started the ignition and driven away from Portland General.

He'd had no doubt he'd get away with this. His mission to discredit Children's Connection was almost complete.

Getting rich was definitely the best revenge.

When Carrie and Brian returned to Portland General around 9:00 p.m., Carrie felt as if they'd landed straight in the midst of a movie set. There were squad cars with flashing lights everywhere.

Brian drove into the parking garage and found more officers, two with dogs.

"Do you think there was a bomb threat?" Carrie asked.

"We'll soon find out."

As soon as they exited the car, an officer was there. "What's your business in the hospital?" he asked.

"Our baby's in the nursery."

The officer was silent a moment. Then he asked, "Can I see some ID?"

Carrie felt a knot begin to form in her stomach. She and Brian both showed the policeman their driver's license.

After a thorough search of their faces and their pictures, the cop handed them back. "What are you doing here this late? Visiting hours were over at eight."

Brian put his arm around Carrie, and she was suddenly glad for the additional warmth. He explained, "We're adopting a baby. An infant. He was born today and he's in the nursery. We came to feed him."

A different look came over the policeman's face. He was young, maybe in his midtwenties, and he had black hair, trimmed short, close to his head. His posture became even stiffer. "Is the woman who gave birth to the baby here?"

"Yes," Carrie said quickly, "but we know it's too late to visit her. We just want to hold our son—"

"What's her name?" the officer cut in.

As Brian drew Carrie even closer, she went cold all over. "Her name's Lisa Sanders," Brian answered.

The officer's expression, which before had looked authoritative, now became grim. "I'm going to escort you inside. Detective Levine will want to talk to you."

"Why?" Carrie wanted to know right here and right now what was going on, and why they needed to talk to a police detective.

"Just follow me inside. Detective Levine will explain everything."

Carrie and Brian didn't speak as they hurried across the catwalk and into Portland General. The officer took them to the OB/GYN floor. Everyone looked harried, especially the nurses. As Carrie and Brian passed two who were talking, Carrie heard, "I can't believe it happened here."

What had happened here? a voice inside of Carrie screamed.

Before they reached the nurses' desk, the young police officer escorted them into the lounge. "Wait here," he commanded, then left.

"I'll wait here two minutes," Brian said. "If he's not back, I'll go find out—"

The man who came into the lounge looked as if he'd seen more of life than he'd wanted to see. He was about five-ten, with graying black hair, a crooked nose and a square jaw. He was stocky, and his suit looked rumpled.

When he approached them, he asked, "Brian and Carrie Summers?"

They both nodded.

"I'm Detective Abe Levine." He motioned to the sofa. "I was about to call you when Officer Moreland told me you were here. Why don't you have a seat?"

"Why do we need to sit?" Brian asked, and Carrie could tell he was getting impatient.

"I need to explain a few things to you," the detective responded calmly. "Please. Sit down."

Reluctantly, Brian eased himself down beside Carrie and waited. She could count each beat of her heart because it was pounding so hard.

"We had an incident here tonight. There's no easy way for me to say this. Lisa Sanders's baby—*your* baby—was kidnapped."

"No!" For a moment Carrie's world went black, and she leaned against Brian.

"I know this is a shock. I want you to know we're doing everything possible to find him."

"How could he have been kidnapped?" Brian asked, his voice stony cold. "There's a security code on that nursery. There are residents and nurses and mothers here all the time."

"We haven't figured it all out yet. We're investigating. Asking questions. Getting details. Searching for that one tip that could lead us in the right direction."

"You don't have anything?" Brian asked incredulously.

"We did find something. But we're keeping that evidence quiet. Not letting all the information out often helps us solve the crime. I need to ask you a few questions."

"How's Lisa?" Carrie asked, her thoughts going to the young girl who had become so important to her.

"She's upset. She's scared. I'll let you see her as soon as we're done here."

"When did this happen?" Brian wanted to know, apparently not caring about the detective's questions, but having a multitude of his own.

As if Brian hadn't interrupted, the detective took out

his notebook and glanced at it. "It happened around eight-fifteen." He paused. "You and Mrs. Summers will be adopting this baby. Correct?"

"Yes," Carrie answered.

"Miss Sanders made provisions that if anything happened to her during labor and delivery, the child would go to you."

"Apparently you already know that's so," Brian snapped.

"I need to confirm it."

"Yes, we made those provisions for her," Brian answered. "Lisa was going to sign the adoption documents tomorrow. We couldn't do those until after the baby was born."

"I understand that." The detective consulted his notes again. "The nurses told me you and Mrs. Summers fed the baby at six. What did you do afterward?"

"Are we suspects?" Brian asked.

"This is just routine, Mr. Summers."

Carrie laid her hand on her husband's arm. "Brian and I went out for dinner. We have the charge receipt if you need that. Then we went home and—" Her voice caught. "We were making sure everything was ready in the nursery. I washed bottles. Brian attached the car seat in the car." They'd been so happy, so open with each other, so ready to be parents.

"I know this is hard, Mrs. Summers. Just a few more questions." With steady concentration he stared at Brian. "Do you have any enemies who want to see your life turned upside down?"

"No."

"Don't answer so quickly, Mr. Summers. In the business you're in, I imagine there's competition. Maybe you made a deal or two at the expense of someone else."

"Yes, there's competition, Detective. But all the deals I make are fair and aboveboard. If you need to look through my files, feel free. I don't have anything to hide."

"I might want to do that, but not quite yet." His attention landed on Carrie. "I understand you were once a model."

In a short amount of time, he'd found out a lot about them. "Yes, I was."

"But you're not anymore?"

"No."

"You do volunteer work here?"

"Yes."

"Is anyone here particularly jealous of you? You know, gossips about you, makes snide remarks, maybe feels you have a little bit too much of everything?"

"Not that I know of, Detective."

"I'd like you to do something for me, Mrs. Summers. Make a list of all the charity work you do, and the people you've worked with within the last three months. I know that's going to be tedious, but it might help me. And, Mr. Summers, I'd like the same kind of list from you. Anyone you've worked with, anyone you've bought property from, anyone who's invested with you. I'd also appreciate a list of your employees. The sooner you can get all of this to me, the better."

The detective stood. "I think that about covers it for now."

Carrie rose to her feet, feeling as if her world had just crumbled apart. But she had to get to Lisa. She had to do what she could to comfort her, too.

"I already found out from Miss Sanders that she was

homeless and that Children's Connection hooked you up with her. Can I ask you why you took her into your home?" Levine asked.

"She had no place to go," Carrie replied.

"With due respect, I know you could have put her up in an apartment. Why let her invade your life?"

Carrie knew she'd taken Lisa in to give her own life purpose, but this detective might not understand that. "Lisa needed a place to belong. We gave her that. In return, she was going to give us her baby. It's that simple, Detective."

"She mentioned she might be going to college. Are you paying for that?" His question was aimed at Brian.

"Yes," Brian answered without the anger now. "We'd never be able to repay her for giving us the gift of her child, but college will give her a new life."

Finally the detective closed his notebook and slipped it into his jacket pocket.

"What's your theory on this, Detective?" Brian asked. "You don't have to give me any details, just a hint as to whom you think might have done this."

The detective eyed Brian for a long moment. "If someone didn't do this to hurt you and your wife, if you actually don't have any enemies, then I think someone targeted Miss Sanders. I think they knew she was homeless, didn't have a family, and decided her baby was the one they wanted, either for personal or other reasons. But whoever it was we will find them. And we'll find your baby, too."

Carrie's mind was swimming with all the possibilities of what could have happened. When Brian didn't ask any more questions, she knew his was, too. They were both still trying to absorb the fact that the baby they had already begun to love had disappeared.

There was an expression of absolute sorrow on Brian's face as they walked down the corridor. He looked as if his universe had been blasted, and she knew the feeling. However, his expression changed when they crossed the threshold into Lisa's room. His jaw became sternly set, and his body stance was absolutely taut.

Lisa looked awful. Her eyes were red from crying. Her cheeks were splotchy. Her hair was limp. She looked so different from the girl who had been happy to have her pregnancy over with, so happy to be starting on a new life only hours before.

One glance at Brian and Carrie, and Lisa knew they'd been told. "Is there any news?"

"They're investigating," Brian said in a monotone, then went to Lisa's bedside and took the chair there. "Have you told them everything you know?"

"I don't know anything!"

Carrie watched her husband. He didn't move his gaze from Lisa's. "I have to ask you something, Lisa. Did anything happen on the streets? Did somebody come to you with an offer?"

"What kind of offer?"

"For your baby."

"No." Lisa's shocked face had to be believed.

"And they didn't make a higher offer after they learned *we* were going to adopt?"

"No!" she almost shouted.

Crossing to Brian's side, Carrie laid her hand on his shoulder in stunned supplication. "Brian. Lisa would never do such a thing."

"If she was desperate enough, she would."

Carrie knew when someone was desperate they would do almost anything. Still...

Although Carrie expected anger from Lisa, that wasn't the emotion she saw there now. Rather, the teenager didn't turn away. She didn't become defiant. She just kept staring into Brian's eyes. "I might have been desperate, but I never would have done something like that. Never. I don't want anyone to have this baby but you and Carrie. You've got to believe me."

Normally Brian would analyze information in a situation to come to a decision. But this time Carrie saw the teenager had spoken straight to his heart.

His expression softened as his hand covered Lisa's, and his tone was gentle as he responded, "I believe you."

Tears rolled down Lisa's face, and Brian gave her a hug. "It's going to be okay. The detective says they'll find whoever did this. They'll find Timothy."

"That's what they say on TV," Lisa mumbled into his shoulder. "Sometimes it doesn't happen there, either."

As Carrie sat on the bed by Lisa's hip, she wanted to say they'd all pray for the return of the baby, but she didn't know if she had the right to pray. Not after what she'd done to another child. Her throat was clogged with too many words, her heart swimming in emotions.

When Brian leaned away from Lisa, he said, "I'm going to take a walk and see what else I can find out."

Carrie wanted to plead with him to stay, to hold her, to let her know they'd have a marriage—no matter what happened. But already she was feeling a wall going back up between them. Already a type of resignation was settling over Brian. And she knew what she was going to have to do.

Now she had to find the courage to do it.

Thirteen

"And he was stolen right out of the hospital nursery—with the new security codes and everything!" Nancy Allen explained, her voice trembling with outrage.

The news didn't come as a surprise to Everett, but he pretended to be surprised...and horrified. "This happened tonight?"

"Yes. After visiting hours. I was just getting off my shift when the police cruisers drove up and officers began searching the hospital. Brian and Carrie are going to be sick about this. Absolutely devastated."

"Brian and Carrie Summers? What do they have to do with it?"

"I guess I forgot to mention it to you. They're adopting Lisa Sanders's baby."

Everett swallowed hard at that news. Brian Summers was rich and probably had all kinds of connections.

Composing himself, he replied, "I imagine they'll take the news hard." He put false encouragement into his voice. "Maybe the police will find the baby soon."

"I have this feeling that they'll never find him." Nancy's voice had gone low.

"Why do you say that? Maybe this was a deranged woman who just wants a baby of her own and she didn't go far."

"I don't think a deranged woman would have a key-card and know the security code. I think there's a black-market baby ring at work."

Fear grabbed Everett's heart. "It's a long jump to that conclusion." He didn't want Nancy going down that road.

"I've been hearing things," Nancy said.

"What kind of things?" He tried to keep his voice steady.

"Remember those two couples I told you about who were turned down by the adoption agency?"

Everett's heart was racing now.

"One of the other nurses told me both of them have babies now. How could that have happened so quickly?"

Everett knew exactly how. "Private adoptions occur all the time. Remember, I told you I have a friend who's a lawyer in that field. I spoke to Brian and Carrie Summers about it, but they didn't want to go that route."

"Maybe they should have," Nancy said sadly. "I still think I should go to the police and tell them what I think."

"That's not a good idea. If you do, they could start an investigation into Children's Connection. That'll damage its reputation."

"Its reputation won't mean anything if more of this

goes on. I really think I should talk to the police about this. I'll go in the morning."

Everett felt a noose tightening around his neck. "You can't do that, Nancy!"

"Why not? I—"

Suddenly Everett heard voices in the background on Nancy's end.

She muttered into the phone, "Wait a minute."

There was silence for a few seconds while sweat broke out on his brow.

When she came back she said, "Everett, I've got to go. I thought I was off for the night, but one of the internists has a question about a patient I cared for. I'll talk to you later."

And she was gone.

"Nancy? Nancy?"

She couldn't go to the police. She just couldn't. His head was pounding and he didn't know what to do. He'd had another one of those "visions" earlier. A tall man was clasping his hand. They were in a baseball stadium. He could feel the little-kid excitement of being someplace big and noisy, and seeing real baseball players for the first time. Then the vision…the memory had faded. That man had been his *real* father. Lester Baker, the man who had stolen him, had never taken him to a baseball game.

Everett shook off the memory of a happy life as well as memories of his time with Jolene and Lester Baker… memories of a family that was so dysfunctional it defined the word.

Whatever past pictures his mind held, he didn't have time for them now. He had to call Charlie. He had to find out what to do about Nancy.

Everett had been watching TV on his brown leather couch when Nancy had called. Now, with his cordless phone in hand, he punched in Charlie's cell phone number.

Charlie didn't pick up on the first ring, or the third, and Everett was starting to panic. But then he heard, "Yeah, Baker. Whaddaya want?"

Everett knew Charlie had caller ID and always screened his calls. "Where are you?" Everett wanted to know.

"I'm at my sister's. She's changing the kid now and cooing all over him like she was his mother. What's up? Do you have the name of a couple for me?"

"No. I'm afraid we've got trouble. Nancy's putting too many things together. She suspects somebody took the Sanders kid to make money."

"*How* does she suspect? Unless you told her—"

"I haven't told her anything. Do you think I'm crazy? I don't want to get caught any more than you do. Some nurse told her about couples who got turned down by the agency, then suddenly had babies a month later."

Charlie whistled through his teeth, and then swore. "So who's she talked to about all this?"

"Just me, so far. She wants to go to the police, though. Tomorrow."

Dead silence met his statement, and Everett knew immediately he had done the wrong thing. He never should have called the Stork.

"I'm glad you called me with this, Baker. I'll take care of it. I'll take care of it tonight."

"What are you going to do?"

"What do you think I'm going to do? Don't you worry about Nancy Allen. We'll both be safer without her. Now

I gotta get goin'. You find me another couple, Baker. And find one fast, or I'll be givin' my sister your cut."

At that, the phone went silent.

Fifteen minutes later, as a cold drizzle trickled down his windshield, Everett parked in one of the parking places designated for hospital staff near the emergency room at Portland General and hurried inside, well aware of two squad cars also in the parking lot. This might be the stupidest move he'd ever made. But he couldn't let anything happen to Nancy, and he knew something was going to happen to her tonight if he wasn't with her.

Understanding how dedicated she was to her career, he'd guessed she'd still be at the hospital. And he was right. After he inquired about her at the desk, the nurse on duty pointed down a corridor that led to examination rooms. The nurse, who recognized Everett from his frequent comings and goings to see Nancy, said, "Officially, she's off duty. Remind her she has to get some sleep. She's taking over my shift tomorrow night so I can go to my son's open house at school."

"I'll remind her," Everett answered, having no plan in mind at all.

All he knew was that he had to keep Nancy safe. She was the best thing that had ever happened to him. She was the only person who had ever really listened to him. She didn't seem to mind that he didn't always know what to say, especially to a woman. He'd never had a real relationship before because *before* he'd paid women for the pleasure of sex.

His yearning for Nancy had gotten stronger every time he was with her. In fact, he'd backed away over and over again, at first, to keep himself disentangled from unknown territory, and then for her sake, because of what he'd been doing and what he'd become. Tonight, though, he had to figure out how to stop Charlie and whatever he'd planned to do to Nancy.

Moments later he found her exiting an examination cubicle. As soon as she saw him, she smiled, and in spite of everything that was going on, he felt lighter inside.

"What are *you* doing here?" she asked.

"You sounded upset on the phone. I thought you might get tied up here for hours if there was questioning. Thought you might need some company."

"The police were finished with us before I called you. I should have said something to them then."

"That's one of the reasons I came to pick you up. I want to talk to you about that."

"You came to pick me up?" She looked perplexed.

"I know you're off now, and I thought maybe I could take the day off tomorrow." He could feel a flush crawling up his neck. "I thought I could take you home and—"

"You'll spend the night?" Her eyes were wide. She'd invited him to stay before and he hadn't.

"Yes, I'll stay the night. Then tomorrow, if you want me there—"

"I want you there." Her eyes moistened, and Everett felt his whole heart coming alive in a way it never had before.

In the car, Everett thought about what he should be doing and saying. He'd never known affection, so it was hard for him to show affection. Yet with Nancy, he knew he had to push past the curtain that had always seemed to surround his life and reach for more—even if he only might have it for an hour, or a day, or a week.

With one hand on the steering wheel, he reached

over to her and laid a hand on her knee. "You must be exhausted. You pulled a double shift, didn't you?"

"Yes. But right now I'm anything but tired."

He heard the slight teasing in her voice, the slight edge of seductiveness. That was meant for him.

Ten minutes later, Nancy was using her key to let herself into her apartment. Everett couldn't help but look over his shoulder. Nancy's apartment complex was on the outskirts of Portland. She was on the ground floor, and Everett now saw that as a detriment for security's sake. All of the apartments had sliding glass doors in the back that led into the dining area of the kitchen. There wasn't much he could do to make glass doors really secure.

Taking her to his place wouldn't be much better. Although he wasn't on the ground floor, a fire escape went up the back of his building. It was old, and the window latches weren't that tight. All he could do was protect Nancy during the night and convince her not to go to the police. He'd wrestle with the problem of Charlie in the morning.

As Nancy entered her living room, she picked up a stray newspaper, a mug of tea she'd left on the coffee table. Her apartment was everything his wasn't. She had plants everywhere, from African violets to a potted palm. The love seat and chair were upholstered in a rose-and-green floral print, which added to the feeling of a garden. She had fern-green drapes on the windows. The caramel-colored braided rug on the floor matched the oak furniture, as well as the frames around the Victorian cottage prints on the wall. Nancy's apartment was light and warmth and welcome. His was utilitarian, sparse and empty of the life he felt here.

"I didn't straighten up," she said, looking embarrassed. "I didn't expect to have…company."

Crossing to her, he took the newspaper from her hand and laid it back on the sofa. "You don't have to straighten up for me. I don't care how neat your place is."

A wealth of emotions seemed to cross her face. "I've been waiting for tonight for weeks."

"Then let's not wait any longer."

All the way home in the car, Carrie tried to rehearse words for what she had to say. But words seemed to scatter with thoughts of Lisa…with the idea of Timothy Jacob missing…with the vision of Brian's face when he heard the news.

The rain stopped and started again as they drove. She watched a rivulet travel down the window, her heart trembling with worry about Timothy, her stomach tight with dread because of what came next. She wished for an escape from what she had to do, but she knew the truth had been a long time coming.

Brian hadn't said a word since they'd left the hospital. He parked in the garage, and after they entered the house he reset the security system. What good were security systems?

"How could a baby disappear from a nursery?" she asked him now. "Alarms and codes and the latest technological bells and whistles can't keep anyone safe, can they?"

They'd reached the kitchen when Brian answered, "Maybe it was a *false* sense of security. Someone should have been in that nursery every minute." His hand clenched into a fist and he brought it down on the granite counter.

Crossing to him, Carrie covered his fist with her hand. "Don't. You're only going to hurt yourself."

"I want to wring somebody's neck. I want to be out there on the streets searching myself. Maybe that's what I should do." He checked his watch. "And while I do it, I'll call the private investigator my firm's used in the past for background checks. Maybe he'll find something the police can't."

When Brian would have started for the garage again, she grabbed his arm. "Wait. I have to talk to you."

"Carrie, I know women handle this kind of thing by talking, by going over it again and again. But I have to *do* something."

She released his arm. "I know you do. But please, let me say what I have to say before I lose the courage."

Focused on her, he gave her his full attention now as he stood perfectly still. "Why would you need courage to tell me anything?"

As soon as the words were out of his mouth, something about him changed. His back became ramrod-straight, his eyes narrowed and his mouth was a tight line until he asked, "Are you having an affair? Is that what you're hiding?"

"No! How could you even suspect that of me?"

"Because something hasn't been right between us. Something besides not being able to have a baby."

"Something hasn't been right since the day we got married," she admitted. But when his expression became even grimmer, she hurried to say, "Not that I don't love you, that I didn't love you. I did. And do. And always will."

"Then what is it?" His voice was patient but frustrated…patient but strained on the edge of an emotion she was perched on herself.

There was no way to wrap the truth in a pretty package. The time had come for complete honesty, and she had to just tell him what had happened. "When I was eighteen, I was raped."

It took a few moments for her words to sink in. When they did, he swore. "My God, Carrie. Why didn't you ever tell me?"

"Because there's more."

"More than a woman surviving rape?" He started to reach for her. "So much makes sense now."

She wouldn't let him embrace her and backed away. "Listen to me, Brian. Listen to everything."

When he raked his hand through his hair, she knew he was restraining every impulse inside of him to enfold her into his arms. But she couldn't let him do that yet. When she was done, he might not want to.

"I had just moved to Portland a couple of months before—after graduation. My career had really taken off. I had already done shoots in New York and London, and offers were coming in to my agent every day. I was sending money home, money like my family had never seen. We were able to move out of the poorest section of Windsor to an apartment that was clean and bright with a small garden. It was all like a dream come true, and none of us could believe it. I was just beginning to. Mom and Dad were dreaming about never using food stamps again. Mary and Brenda were dreaming about college. Foolish and naive as I was, I was dreaming about more magazine covers and traveling…visiting the French Riviera."

"Carrie," he said softly.

She shook her head. "But then I was walking home after a shoot one night. A few blocks from my apartment, he grabbed me. He was wearing a ski mask. I fought him but—" She stopped for a second then went on. "Somehow, I made it to my apartment, but then something happened to me. I spiraled down into a black hole. Mom came and got me and took me home, but we didn't tell anyone—not Dad, not my sisters, not anyone. Dad knows now. Mom just told him recently, but—" She swallowed hard. "Once Mom took me home, I couldn't sleep. I couldn't eat. I just stayed in bed and cried. A few weeks afterward I missed my period."

Now Brian looked stunned. She realized she was delivering blow after blow, but it all had to come out, every single sordid bit of it.

"You were pregnant," he stated flatly.

"Yes. And everything was on the line—my family's life, my future and my career."

She could make excuses, but she wasn't going to. This was her responsibility. "Through the grapevine, Mom had heard of a doctor who performed abortions. I went to him. A week later I had a fever of one hundred five and he put me on antibiotics. I didn't know then—" Her voice caught and she stopped.

"Didn't know what?" Brian prodded.

"I didn't know the infection was more extensive than I'd ever dreamed. I didn't know I'd never be able to have children—until we couldn't get pregnant and I went to the specialist."

Shell-shocked. Brian looked absolutely shell-shocked.

"When we got married, I wanted a baby as much as you did. I didn't know, Brian. You've *got* to believe me."

He looked away, then his gaze returned to hers and seemed to pierce right through her. "But there was the medical report…about your tubes being blocked."

"That was accurate. There had been scarring—extensive scarring. That's probably why in vitro didn't work, either."

"The doctor knew about all of this?"

"I had to tell him. I had to know for sure what our chances were. He said we had a chance, but then it didn't work—"

"And still you didn't tell me." Brian sounded so pained, so betrayed.

He had a right to everything he was feeling. There was only one thing she could do. "You deserve to be married to a woman who can give you children. You didn't sign on for this. If I had been truthful with you from the beginning, maybe we would have never gotten married. Maybe we would have considered adoption sooner if we had. This whole situation with Lisa never would have happened. I want to find Timothy Jacob with all my heart, and I still want to adopt him. But I can understand if you don't want to be part of that. I understand that keeping all of this from you, and the abortion itself, might be too much to forgive."

Brian's expression was absolutely unreadable. She wished he'd say something, anything, but he didn't. She knew how he felt about right and wrong, black and white, taking the high road. She represented a blurring of everything he believed in. She wasn't the woman she'd portrayed to him, and she'd been right to think their marriage could never recover from the truth of it all. Brian's silence told her more than words. There *was* only one thing to do.

"I'm going to pack a suitcase and go to a hotel tonight."

"It's late," he protested.

"I know. I'll go to the Ambassador. I'll be fine. We both need time to think about everything."

"I have to call the private investigator and search for Timothy," Brian said, as if the rest of it were secondary. She supposed it was just too much to take in. Searching for the baby they'd lost seemed simpler.

"I won't be here when you get back," she said.

Brian's gaze swept over her. Then, as if he couldn't stand to look at her another second, he left the kitchen and went to the garage. She heard his car door slam. She heard him start the engine. She heard him drive away.

Finally letting all the emotion come to the surface, she felt a sob tear through her, and tears began falling down her cheeks. She had to leave. She wouldn't be able to stay, living with the guilt of what she'd done, seeing recriminations in Brian's eyes. Seeing hurt…and pain.

Everett lay in bed with Nancy, curled spoon-fashion, his arm around her. She was warm, her skin was soft, and her hair smelled like strawberries. They had made love twice. The first time he'd felt like a fumbling idiot, and she'd made it easy. She'd even made putting on the condom a new adventure. The second time they'd made love, it had seemed natural. His climax had hit the same time as hers. Nothing had mattered except being inside of her, being with her.

Still, it couldn't last.

Tightening his hold on Nancy, he let his thoughts drift as he dozed. They were a mixture of good and bad, past and present, but no future.

Suddenly he went on alert. There was a noise. The glass doors opening?

Slipping out of bed, he was glad to see Nancy was still asleep. She'd been exhausted after her double shift in the E.R. The parking lot's light came through the edges of the blind. Everett scooped up the first solid heavy object he saw. It was a sculpture of a cat done in bronze. Hoisting it to his shoulder, he was ready to throw it at anything that moved. Going through the living room, he saw a figure dressed in black in the kitchen.

He flattened himself against the inside wall and waited. There was one step, and then another. As he brought up the sculpture, he took a huge breath. When the figure stepped through the doorway, he brought it down solidly, clipping the man's shoulder. There was a grunt, then a parry, as a gun fell out of the man's hand and flew almost at Everett's feet. He could see it in the light of the street lamp coming in the window.

The man in black swore. "Hell, Baker, is that you?"

Everett realized it was the Stork himself, and not some henchman he'd hired. His voice was a low threat. "Get out of here, Charlie. I'm not going to let you hurt her."

Charlie's eyes darted to the gun, but Everett scooped it up before the man could even think about doing it. He pointed it at his once-friend. "You are *not* going to hurt her. Get out of here before she wakes up."

"What if she goes to the police?" Charlie hissed.

"If she does, I'll discredit her somehow. Trust me, Charlie. I'll handle it. If you get any ideas about hurting me, as well as Nancy…" He hefted up the gun in his hand. "Well, I've got this now. And I'll use it."

Charlie gazed at him with something Everett had never seen in his eyes before—respect.

"Everett? Is that you? Is something wrong?" Nancy called from the bedroom.

"Get out of here," he ordered Charlie.

Without his gun, all Charlie could do was snarl.

"You'd better fix this, Baker. You'd better fix it right." Then he scuttled to the kitchen.

"It's just me, Nancy," Everett called into the bedroom. "I thought I heard something, but it must have been the rain and the wind."

Once Charlie was gone, Everett locked the door behind him, then he didn't know why he bothered. Locked doors weren't going to keep Charlie out—not if he really wanted to get in. But Everett had felt the balance of power shift a little bit tonight.

After stowing the gun behind a large vase in the china cabinet, Everett carried the bronze cat back into the bedroom. He'd retrieve the gun in the morning while Nancy was taking her shower.

"What were you doing with *that?*" Nancy asked, sitting up in bed.

"I was going to use it on an intruder." He managed a smile.

She patted the bed beside her. "Come back to bed."

First he turned off the light, set down the cat, then he crawled into bed.

When they faced each other, she declared, "I'm going to the police tomorrow, Everett. I have to. If I'm right about this, maybe we can save other couples heartache. I can only imagine what Brian and Carrie are going through tonight."

Everett had fallen for Nancy Allen because she was the woman she was—caring, compassionate and much too good for him. "I'll go with you," he assured her, already planning damage control, already working out a strategy to keep both of them alive.

Fourteen

At 5:00 a.m. Brian entered the bedroom he'd shared with Carrie and sank down onto the chair in the sitting area. All night he'd driven the streets, as well as walked them in the rain, not even knowing what he was looking for. A baby carriage? Squad cars surrounding a row house, a policeman exiting with Timothy Jacob in his arms?

As he dropped his head in his hands, he told himself the police were doing everything they could. Plus, his private investigator was on the case now.

He'd turned on a small bedside lamp when he'd entered the room. Now the darkness and shadows, and especially the silence, surrounded him. There'd been a deep, yawning ache in his gut ever since Carrie had told him—

Carrie.

Why had everything gone so monumentally wrong? Why had she kept something so huge from him? The biggest question of all gnawed at him. Why hadn't she trusted him enough to tell him?

Rape. Abortion. Infertility. She'd kept it hidden so well, he hadn't suspected. Or had he? Hadn't he always known she was holding back? Hadn't he always guessed there was a reason? Why hadn't he pursued it? Why hadn't he prodded her? Why hadn't he gotten to the bottom of it?

From the first night he'd laid eyes on Carrie, he'd known he'd wanted her as his. Their whirlwind courtship had led into marriage and a honeymoon and then—and then his push for a family.

When had their marriage stopped being about *them?*

Why hadn't they continued to get to know each other and grow together?

That answer was easy. Carrie had walls. He had walls. He'd let work be the balm, the basis and the ballast of his life. He'd thought he'd put Carrie in the center. In an odd way he had, but he'd never joined her there. He always orbited around her. Maybe he was as afraid as she was of what would happen if they became truly intimate…intimate in their hearts and emotions, not only with their bodies.

He needed some answers, and he needed them from a different perspective than Carrie's. He needed to talk to her mother.

Without even thinking about a shower and ignoring the emptiness in his stomach, he hurried to his car once more and set off for Windsor.

Less than ninety minutes later, he pulled up in front of the house where Paula and George Bradley lived, just now realizing they might not even be up.

However, after he climbed the porch steps, he didn't

even have to ring the bell. The door opened and George stood there in a flannel shirt and jeans, without looking a bit surprised. "Carrie called her mama last night."

"I need some answers."

"Don't know how I can help with that. You and Carrie have to find the answers together."

"If she called, then you know she left."

"She left because that's what she thought you'd want her to do."

Brian swore and rubbed the back of his neck.

George opened the door wider. "You look pretty rough. Come on in. I've already got the first pot of coffee on."

Although Brian had been in the Bradley house many times before, he looked at it with fresh eyes. It wasn't extravagant by any means. But he could feel warmth in this home, as well as family connections—intangible bonds that he was finding out were so much more important than plush carpeting or the best furniture money could buy. He knew Carrie's mom no longer cleaned houses. Carrie had put a sum of money aside for her parents, and they lived off of the investment income. Paula now worked as a cashier in the local drugstore. But she still cut coupons. The Bradleys might depend on their daughter, but they'd kept their self-respect.

George poured two mugs of coffee. "Paula's not up yet. She was talking to Carrie on the phone pretty late. Carrie told her about the kidnapping, too. You must feel like a freight train bowled you over."

Brian wasn't sure what he thought or what he felt. "Carrie said she didn't tell you about the rape at first."

George's only reaction to Brian's bluntness was an arched brow. He set one of the mugs of coffee before Brian on the table. "You take it black, right?"

Brian nodded.

George hobbled to the table, his stiff leg making his gait uneven. After he eased himself into the chair, he took the warm coffee mug into his hands. "Nope. Carrie never told me. I didn't know about it officially until about a week ago. Paula filled me in. Said she couldn't keep it a secret from me anymore."

"After all these years." Brian shook his head.

"Fear's a great motivator, boy. Fear can keep a man or woman silent for almost a decade. It can make them do things they wouldn't ever do otherwise."

"You mean the abortion?"

"I mean all of it. Did Carrie tell you her mama made all the arrangements? Her mama told her over and over again it was the best thing to do. Her mama told her it was the only way she would have a future, the only way we'd survive."

"No." Brian felt the word echo through his whole being. Carrie had taken full responsibility, and he suspected why.

"Carrie was a mess that summer," George went on. "I knew something was wrong, but I didn't poke around. Her mom said she was sick from exhaustion, but I was too deep into painkillers back then, too deep into feeling sorry for myself. Paula was desperate. Do you understand she gave Carrie the only option she thought we had?"

"Take me through it, will you?" Brian asked, still attempting to piece it together. "Give me as much as you know."

George related everything Paula had told him about the rape, and how she'd arranged the abortion. Then he said, "And even after the doctor gave Carrie medicine and her fever broke, she wasn't the same. She wouldn't leave her bedroom. She wouldn't even talk to Whitney or Brenda or Mary. She lost ten pounds. Paula took her back to Portland and found her a counselor. After she went to sessions every day with her for a week, Carrie began to come around. But even after Paula came home, she called her two, three times a day to make sure she was okay. I remember when Carrie came here for Thanksgiving that year. She'd put some weight back on and was beginning to look like her old self. By then she'd told her agent the basics and he eased her back into working with safe assignments. Then she got that Modern Woman Cosmetics contract, and she seemed to be okay."

When Brian heard a noise in the doorway, he looked over his shoulder. Paula Bradley was standing there in a gray sweatsuit. She didn't look surprised to see him, either.

"Hello, Brian."

"Paula." He'd always been on the fringes of Carrie's family. Why hadn't he gotten to know them better? Why hadn't he become really integrated into their lives? He didn't like the picture forming of the man he'd been.

Paula brushed her hair away from her face, a gesture similar to one of Carrie's.

Opening the refrigerator, she took out a pitcher of orange juice and poured herself a glass. "Carrie was in counseling for over two years," she said, picking up the conversation she'd obviously been listening to.

"It apparently helped," Brian said. "I never guessed something so traumatic had happened to her."

"She worked hard at overcoming it all. The anger. The pain. The violation. Probably a lot of resentment toward me."

"She doesn't resent you," he said automatically.

"She *did*. What I made her do came between us until just recently. I think that's because of adopting the baby."

After Paula sat at the table with them, silence filled every corner of the kitchen.

"Why didn't she tell me?" Brian asked, knowing most of the answer, but trying to discover if there was more.

"Did she ever mention Foster Garrett?" Paula asked him.

"No. Who was that?"

"He was the first man she dated when she was ready to date again."

Brian hated the thought of Carrie being connected to another man. "Was it serious?"

"Carrie was serious," Paula admitted. "But when she told Foster about the rape and the abortion, he decided he didn't want to see her anymore. She'd come home one weekend after the breakup, and I could see something was troubling her. She said the tone of his voice after she explained all of it told her she was damaged goods, not fit for someone like him. Was that the impression you gave her last night? Is that why she left?"

There was anger in Paula's tone, and Brian knew if he had been Carrie's parent, he'd be angry, too. "I honestly don't know what impression I gave her. We'd just gotten home after talking to the detective. She just let it all spill out. I was angry, hurt, feeling betrayed."

"Betrayed?" Paula's voice was harsher now. "Carrie never did anything to betray you. She was trying to *protect* you. Granted, she was trying to protect herself, too, and her marriage."

George laid his hand on Paula's on the table. "Easy."

"She's right, George," Brian decided. "I've been

blind. Most of all, I've been stupid. I married this wonderful, beautiful, intelligent woman, and I never took the time to really know her. I never delved into why she was afraid of the dark or why our security system was so important to her. I let her pick and choose what she wanted to tell me about her modeling career. I didn't pry into past relationships. I should have done all those things. I should have cared enough to want to do all those things."

Paula pushed her juice away and sighed. "You're a good man, Brian. You're driven to succeed. You have a moral code that's admirable, but if anyone falls short of your standards, you cut her from your life."

Paula was talking about his mother and holding up a mirror of how he'd self-righteously viewed the world. What had Lisa said about mothers? *I don't have one anymore and I wish I did.* He had one, and he couldn't be man enough to forgive her. Carrie had seen that. She had seen too much. She had seen his inflexibility, his desire to succeed, his lack of trust in her. She'd been right about that. He'd kept himself from becoming emotionally intimate because he was afraid she would leave. So what had he done? He'd driven her away.

I want her back.

He was as certain of that as he was that he needed air to breathe. He needed Carrie in his life. Life didn't mean a damn thing without her. More than need, he loved her to the very bottom of his soul. He hadn't told her that often, either. Yes, he'd told her that he wanted her, but not that he loved her. Now he wasn't just going to have to tell her. He was going to have to show her.

"I've got to go." He pushed back his chair.

"To Carrie?" George asked.

"I have something I have to do first. But then, yes, I'm going to her. Somehow, I'm going to convince her to give me another chance."

When he stood, he told the Bradleys, "I promise you, no one means more to me than your daughter. Nothing means more to me than Carrie. I love her, and I'm going to spend the rest of my life proving it."

Paula stood, too, and there was encouragement on her face and a bit of a twinkle in her eye. "Before you go see her, you'd better shave and clean up a bit. You'll scare her to death if you don't."

Rubbing his hand over his beard stubble, glancing at his wrinkled shirt and his damp jeans, he nodded. "I'll make sure I do that."

Then Paula hugged him, and George gave him a grin.

Brian had found a family that had been waiting for him all along.

The detective's office was smaller than Everett would have expected. But at least it had a door that closed. Nancy was waiting outside. He'd simply told her there were a few things he wanted to ask the detective about the investigation man-to-man, and she'd accepted that.

Now Levine asked him, "What did you want to talk to me about, Mr. Baker?"

"About Nancy Allen's suggestion that this is some kind of black-market operation. I don't think anything could be farther from the truth."

"Why do you say that?" Levine casually leaned back in his chair.

"Because Children's Connection is an A-plus organization with no one but the best people running it. Besides that, you've got to understand the strain Nancy's been under."

"Strain?"

"She's an E.R. nurse. Last night she'd worked a double shift. She does a lot of that, and she was exhausted when this kidnapping happened. It affected a close friend of hers, Carrie Summers. She's overwrought with the repercussions and the heartache of it. I think you ought to take that into consideration in any statements she makes."

Levine studied Everett, and then made a note in the file on his desk. "All right. I'll give your comments due consideration. Is there anything else we need to discuss?"

Everett knew he had to be careful. If he came on too heavy, or undermined Nancy too much, Levine might get suspicious of *him*. "No. That's it. I don't want to take up any more of your time. I do hope you find the Sanders baby soon…for everybody's sake."

Standing before the hotel room door, Brian knocked. He'd called Carrie from the lobby, gotten her room number and told her he was coming up. She hadn't protested, and he hoped that was a good sign. When he'd returned from Carrie's parents, there had been a phone message from Lisa, saying she was being discharged. She wanted to know what she should do. He'd known exactly what *he* should do. He'd told her to sit tight, and he'd be there as soon as he ran an errand.

Now Lisa was waiting back at the house. He was hoping he'd be bringing his wife home to help console the teenager, to give her hope that Timothy would be found.

When Carrie opened the door, it was easy to see she'd been crying. Even with her nose slightly red, and blue tinges under her eyes, she was the most beautiful woman he'd ever seen.

She avoided his gaze, but said, "I called the hospital to see how Lisa was doing. They said you picked her up. Where is she?"

"She's home."

"Home?"

"At our house, Carrie. At our house."

At that his wife's gaze met his. "Is it still our house? We're not together anymore—" Her voice caught, and she looked away again. "I can take Lisa home. To Mom and Dad's. That way you don't have to look after her."

"Stop writing the script for me, Carrie." The firmness of his voice brought her gaze to his once more.

She'd reserved a simple double room, instead of a suite. Now he took her arm and guided her to one of the beds, bringing his package along. "Sit," he gently commanded.

The way she looked at him almost broke his heart. It was a look full of despair and guilt and self-blame.

Setting the package on the bed behind him, he turned to her and took her hands. "I think you're the most remarkable woman I've ever met."

"Brian…"

"Keep your eyes on mine, Carrie. I want you to hear every word of this and understand it."

When he was sure she wasn't going to try to evade him again, he continued, "You're remarkable because you're a survivor. You've not only survived, but you've survived with courage and beauty and character."

Tears welled up in her eyes, and she shook her head. "I lied to you by not telling you. I never should have had the abortion."

"I talked to your mother this morning—and your

dad—and they tell it a little differently. They told me your mom only gave you one choice. And you weren't in any condition to think of another. First and foremost, Carrie, if we're going to have the wonderful marriage I want us to have, you have to forgive yourself. What's done is done. It's in the past. You can't undo it. But you can learn from it and help others because of it. You're already doing that. You do it with the kids at the hospital, and you're doing it with Lisa."

"I've carried this for so long."

"I know. It's time to let go of it. I want you to let go of it and hold on to me."

Tears were falling down her cheeks now. "How can you forgive me? You want children. If Timothy isn't found—"

"I want *you,* Carrie. Maybe I was never clear enough about that. Maybe I never realized how completely I mean that. The night you were in your accident, I almost lost you. I came to several realizations then. One of them was that you had to be happy. I thought that making you happy meant giving you a huge house, unlimited charge cards, the raciest car in town. I haven't been listening to you. I haven't been listening to what you're *not* saying, as well as what you *do* say. That's going to change. I love you, Carrie Bradley Summers. You are my reason for living, and working, and building a future. Without you, none of it matters."

"Oh, Brian."

The way she said his name squeezed his heart. "Do you love me? Can you forgive the man I was and help teach me to be the man I want to be?"

"I love you, Brian. Just the way you are. I've merely wanted more of you."

"I know what that means now. I really do. We have to have time together to *be* together. And when we *are* together..." He put his arm around her and brought her close. "I want to know what you're thinking and feeling. I want to know all the things you've never told me. I want to know your hopes and dreams and fears."

Turning her face to him, she whispered, "And I want to know yours."

When his lips met Carrie's, the happiness inside him seemed much too unlimited to confine. He expressed it to her with every stroke of his tongue, with each beat of his heart, with every fervent taste of what true intimacy could be between them.

When he broke away he said, "I have something for you."

"You've just given me everything I've ever wanted."

"Not yet." He grinned. "But soon." Then he put the package on her lap.

He could see her fingers were trembling as she unwrapped it. He'd pulled some strings, but he'd managed to get the sketch framed.

As she revealed it, she gasped. "It's *us*. And it has your signature on it."

"I found out I can draw more than buildings when I put my heart into it."

She traced her fingers over the waterfall. Over their faces. Over his name. "Thank you. It's the most wonderful gift I've ever received."

Brian took the framed sketch, laid it beside him and drew Carrie into his arms again. "*You're* the most precious gift *I've* ever received. I love you, Carrie."

"I love you, too," she whispered, then raised her face to his for another kiss.

Epilogue

The last day of January in Windsor, Oregon, was sunny and filled with promise in spite of the anguish in Carrie's heart—in the past few days Timothy still had not been found.

Every day, she, Brian and Lisa prayed that he would be returned soon. Carrie's prayers felt true now, without the guilt she'd carried for so long, without the secrecy that had been tying her down. Brian's unconditional acceptance and love had freed her and had allowed her to free herself. Now she felt ready to give herself to Brian—again. This time for a lifetime.

Brilliant sun streamed through the stained glass windows as she stood at the back of the church with her father. This recommitment ceremony had been Brian's idea. Now, as one of her favorite hymns played in the background, she looked down the chapel's aisle to her husband.

"Let's go," her dad murmured, giving her arm a squeeze.

The ivory satin dress that she'd worn on their honeymoon was perfect for today. The fabric flowed around her as she walked down the aisle.

Lisa, Carrie's mom, dad and sisters, their husbands and children, as well as Leigh and Adam, were their special guests. Carrie hadn't been able to reach Katie, and Nancy hadn't been able to find anyone to cover for her on such short notice.

As Carrie walked toward her husband, she could see the same emotion in his eyes that she was feeling. This time they were going to be united as one. This time they were going to give themselves completely to each other.

Before they'd gotten dressed for the ceremony, Brian had told her he'd called his mother. She was flying in to visit them the following weekend. Carrie hoped for the best. She hoped for the best with everything now. They had discovered so much over the past month, they had found so much. She'd developed a new closeness with her parents and so had Brian. They'd become surrogate parents to Lisa. In a few weeks they'd be moving into the new house with her until she went to college in June. When Timothy Jacob was found—Carrie had to believe he would be—he'd add joy and light to their lives, too. They were surrounded by family and whatever happened in the future, they would be a family.

With each step up the aisle—Carrie had told her dad to take his time—she counted her blessings. When she reached Brian and her dad put her hand in his, she smiled up at her husband, proud to be standing beside him.

After the gray-haired reverend welcomed everyone

to their recommitment ceremony, he said to Brian, "I understand you have something to say to Carrie."

Carrie's father had taken her flowers for her mom to hold. Now as Brian took both of her hands, she gazed up into his eyes.

"I, Brian Summers, take you, Carrie Bradley Summers, to be my wife. I vow to love, honor and cherish you each and every day. I promise I will be dependable, responsible, understanding and forgiving. I want to be your life partner, your friend, your confidant and your lover forever. To the best of my ability I will be your shelter, your home and your comfort. You are the best thing that ever happened to me, Carrie. Every day I will prove how much I appreciate that, how much I appreciate having you in my life. Today I pledge to you my trust with all my heart and soul."

The reverend glanced at Carrie.

She took a deep breath and began, "Our journey has led us here to this place, and we realize and appreciate what we have. Your love is a gift. You *are* my love, Brian, and I vow to stand beside you, to support you, to encourage you, to compromise with you and to love you every day of our lives. You've accepted me for who I am, and I unconditionally accept you, too. I promise to always share my secrets and dreams with you, to trust you and respect you. My heart, soul and body are yours until the end of time."

The reverend looked out at the guests. "Since this couple has already exchanged rings, now they'd like to exchange something else. Carrie."

The reverend handed Carrie a masculine-looking gold watch. Taking Brian's hand, she slipped the watch onto his wrist and clasped it. "Every minute that ticks by, know that my love for you grows stronger." On the back of the watch Carrie had had inscribed, *Beginning Again, Love Always, Carrie.*

Out of his pocket Brian took a delicate bracelet with a solid gold heart at its center. Taking her hand, he fastened it on her wrist. "Every time you look at this bracelet, know that my heart is yours." He whispered in her ear, "It's engraved with something really original—*All My Love, Brian.*" He caressed her cheek as he leaned away.

The reverend was grinning. "Brian and Carrie have recommitted themselves to each other, and with my blessing, I hope you will also give them yours."

After he gave the blessing, he smiled and nodded.

When Brian took Carrie into his arms, the reverend, the church and their guests all faded away. She was his and he was hers.

Forever.

* * * * *

*Turn the page for a sneak preview of the next
emotional LOGAN'S LEGACY title,*

CHILD OF HER HEART

*by reader favorite Cheryl St.John
on sale in December 2004...*

One

Leaving Portland, Meredith Malone drove west along the Sunset Highway. Sweeping wheat fields bordered by verdant hills and towering mountains soon gave way to orchards, which gave way to forests of spruce, alder, cedar and hemlock. In places the highway cut in so deeply that the bases of the huge trees were eye level on both sides of the car, giving the feeling that she was an infinitesimal part of the endless forest. She drove in the shaded wilderness for an hour before seeing sunlight and sky again.

Here, an occasional gift shop dotted the sides of the road, joined by deserted fruit stands that would be busy in later months. During the summer even antique dealers displayed goods along this stretch of road, and tourists with RVs, towing ATVs or with bike and surfboard carriers slowed traffic considerably. This time of year, however, hers was one of only a few cars, so she made good time.

She descended the last hill from Saddle Mountain, pleased that she'd planned the drive for after her three-month-old daughter had been fed and was ready to sleep most of the morning.

She drove through a small river valley and climbed through the dense foliage along the coast. She hadn't been to the coast for years, and as she started the last descent toward Cannon Beach junction, the Pacific Ocean appeared, vast and surprisingly familiar. Ahead was a fleeting distant view of Haystack Rock, projecting a couple of hundred feet out of the water. From almost untouched countryside, she drove the steep loop down to Cannon Beach and into the small town.

From her car seat in the rear, Anna woke and let Meredith know she was hungry with tiny rooting sounds and a long wail of complaint.

"We're there, sweetie. Mommy just has to find the address."

She glanced at the piece of paper on the seat beside her and followed directions through the quaint little community to a multicolored brick inn near the beach. White shutters made the windows look welcoming, and each guest suite sported a sunny balcony. Shrubs bordered the building and lined the drive and the walk.

Meredith unfastened the carrier, grabbed Anna's bag and her purse, and carried the seat holding her baby. She would come back later for the rest of her belongings. Traveling with an infant was an enormous task. She had packed diapers and clothing and blankets and toys, and still she'd wondered if she'd remembered every-thing she would need for her stay. Once again she said a prayer of thanks for the blessing and ability to breast-feed. At least she didn't have to worry about bottles.

It may have been a perfectly natural thing to a million women, but for her it was a gift she never took for granted.

Anna was red-faced and wailing by the time Meredith entered the lobby, set the carrier on the carpeted floor and checked in.

"Sorry," she said above the crying to the woman at the counter. "She's hungry."

The woman nodded. "Can I help you carry your things to your room? Maybe she'll settle down if you take her out and hold her."

"You're probably right." Meredith leaned over, unbuckled Anna's restraints and picked her up. Anna immediately quieted as she peered at her new surroundings and blinked at her mother.

"You've been cooped up in that seat for a while, haven't you, sweetie?" Meredith smiled and turned back for the room key.

The clerk was staring at Anna.

Pain stabbed Meredith's chest. Anna was a beautiful child with black hair, near-black eyes, and velvety skin the color of coffee with cream. Meredith, on the other hand, was as fair-skinned as could be.

Would she ever get used to people staring at the two of them? She waited for a question—people often blurted the first thing on their minds. But this woman displayed a modicum of tact and said nothing.

With a cheerful smile pasted on her face, she came around the wall from the little room she'd been standing in and picked up the carrier and Meredith's bag. "I'll show you to your room."

Not "what a pretty baby" or "what is her name?" Meredith tamped down the hurt as the woman walked her down a hallway and led her to a set of double doors. Meredith used the plastic key card and let herself in. The hotel employee set her belongings just inside. "Have a nice stay."

"Thank you." Meredith closed the door and locked it. Her first impression was that the suite was as large as her apartment at home, but far more elegantly furnished.

Anna was fussing again, so without taking time to investigate the rooms, she hurried to the bedroom, placed the baby on the king-sized bed and changed her diaper. Then Meredith unbuttoned her shirt, settled on a comfortable overstuffed chair and placed Anna at her breast.

Dark eyes looked at her trustingly, smooth dark skin and lips a vivid contrast against Meredith's scarred white breast. She touched her baby's face and smiled. The drive had been beautiful and relaxing, but she was tired from packing and planning and following directions. She kicked off her shoes and propped her feet on a matching ottoman.

The past few months had been tension-filled and emotionally draining. No, the past couple of *years* had been tension-filled and emotionally draining. But the recent months had been worse, rife with her mother's constant disapproval and pressuring. Every time Meredith thought about her mother's reactions, renewed hurt knifed through her heart. Breathing deeply, she worked to fight back her anger before her tension seeped through to the baby in her arms.

Meredith's mother had wanted her to give Anna up for adoption. Meredith wouldn't hear of it. She'd loved her baby from conception. She'd adored her on sight and cherished her more every day since.

But Veronica was embarrassed. She'd been mortified when her daughter gave birth to an African-American child. She wanted the world to know Anna's birth was not by choice or by natural means and she threatened at every opportunity to feed the information about the mistake made by Children's Connection to the media in hopes of having the public's sympathy.

Veronica's obvious shame hurt Meredith more than she could say. She'd been surprised when she'd seen her baby, yes, of course. But ashamed? Certainly not. She was tired of fighting her mother on every front and constantly heading off her confrontations and insistence that Meredith sue Children's Connection. This was her *mother!* She should accept Meredith's decisions and *love* her grandchild.

Tears stung her eyelids and she determinedly blinked them away. She needed this time away from everything—especially from Veronica. She craved privacy. She was looking forward to peace and quiet, time alone with Anna without pressure or censure.

For a few blessed weeks, she wouldn't have to cook or clean; she'd have attendants to help tote and carry. She could see the local sights at her leisure and return here whenever she wanted to put her feet up and do nothing.

She glanced around the elegantly appointed room. This was just the getaway she needed.

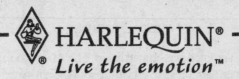

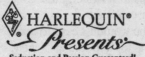

V *Silhouette*

SPECIAL EDITION™

Emotional, compelling stories that capture the intensity of living, loving and creating a family in today's world.

Special Edition features bestselling authors such as Nora Roberts, Susan Mallery, Sherryl Woods, Christine Rimmer, Joan Elliott Pickart— and many more!

For a romantic, complex and emotional read, choose Silhouette Special Edition.

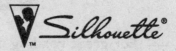
V *Silhouette*®

HARLEQUIN®
Presents

The world's bestselling romance series...
The series that brings you your favorite authors,
month after month:

Helen Bianchin...Emma Darcy
Lynne Graham...Penny Jordan
Miranda Lee...Sandra Marton
Anne Mather...Carole Mortimer
Susan Napier...Michelle Reid

and many more uniquely talented authors!

Wealthy, powerful, gorgeous men...
Women who have feelings just like your own...
The stories you love, set in exotic, glamorous locations...

HARLEQUIN®
Presents

Seduction and Passion Guaranteed!

HPDIR104

From first love to forever, these love stories
are fairy tale romances for today's woman.

Modern, passionate reads that are powerful and provocative.

SPECIAL EDITION™

Emotional, compelling stories that capture the intensity
of living, loving and creating a family in today's world.

A roller-coaster read that delivers romantic thrills
in a world of suspense, adventure and more.

HARLEQUIN®
INTRIGUE®

WE'LL LEAVE YOU BREATHLESS!

If you've been looking for thrilling tales of contemporary passion and sensuous love stories with taut, edge-of-the-seat suspense—then you'll love Harlequin Intrigue!

Every month, you'll meet six new heroes who are guaranteed to make your spine tingle and your pulse pound. With them you'll enter into the exciting world of Harlequin Intrigue— where your life is on the line and so is your heart!

THAT'S INTRIGUE—
ROMANTIC SUSPENSE
AT ITS BEST!

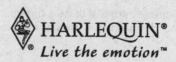

HARLEQUIN®
Live the emotion™